A SHOT OF FREEDOM

Already there were torches coming down the hill, perhaps a quarter mile behind—Coburn and his men. Beard sprinted downslope, came to the mud-and-sand beach, and quickly found his duffel, pulled it open, withdrew his pepperbox pistol. He crouched there, waited, saw them coming ever closer. Beard set his pistol's hammer and said a short prayer.

Then noise and the odor of gunsmoke. Petty Officer Coburn, no more than a hundred feet away at this instant and faintly visible, was yelling at the top of his lungs, at the same time clutching his forearm.

Now it's a hanging offense, Willy thought, but a man had to take his chances if he wanted freedom. . . .

SIERRA SANTA CRUZ

BILL HOTCHKISS

BANTAM BOOKS
NEW YORK · TORONTO · LONDON · SYDNEY · AUCKLAND

SIERRA SANTA CRUZ

A Bantam Domain Book / January 1992

ISBN 0-553-29556-X

Published simultaneously in the United States and Canada

PRINTED IN THE UNITED STATES OF AMERICA

RAD   0 9 8 7 6 5 4 3 2 1

For Ray Oliva,
a man I have been proud to call friend
this past quarter century and more—
a master teacher
an inspiration to many,
one who has demanded excellence
from his students
and has forced those students to perceive
they were capable of excellence.

Contents

SIERRA SANTA CRUZ

Strip Jumper

1

Ship Jumper

Cormorants drifted above the calm waters of Bahía del San Francisco, and the springtime air was rich with life—a sense of fecundity, of generation, of springtime already in progress. Occasional faintly-heard guitar chords blended with the slapping of wavelets against the hull of the *Baltimore Pride*, bound for the British post at Fort Astoria and then on to Nova Archangelisk in Russian Alaska, to trade for the skins of sea otter and Arctic fox.

On shipboard, twenty-seven-year-old William Beard dreamed of Vermont woods and the days of his boyhood—of maples, oaks, pines, and spruces—of the solitude of walking amidst trees, rifle in hand—and the animals, sensing this new malign presence that had been on previous occasions merely a boy ambling through the forest, fled from him. But there in a clearing ahead stood an Indian girl, black hair gleaming in sunlight. . . .

Had it been merely a dream? Indeed, was there some mystically defined point beyond which one simply could not distinguish dream from non-dream? In any case, this fixed idea had been with him for quite a while now, through the years of growing toward manhood and then into manhood itself. Thus, in retrospect, he realized he'd set out to discover in the wide reaches of the world what, at some intuitive level, he'd always *known was there*.

The urge to wander had not been generated, certainly not, by the fact that he'd found the charms of Christie O'Brien unappealing. They'd discovered ample opportunities to meet and kiss, and, for public consumption, often attended church together. But to marry Christie meant responsibilities—and shouldn't a young man such as himself have the opportunity to see the world before he indentured himself to fate?

In the woods of Vermont, New Hampshire, and the District of Maine, he'd worked with his father—and had learned the trade of felling. The handle of a broad-bladed axe fit easily into his hands, and the corded strength of young muscles supplied the rest. Older loggers winked at Bill Beard Senior, spat streams of tobacco juice onto the ground, and opined that *Yore kid's going to put us all to shame as soon's he grows into his corks*.

William Beard the Younger wiped perspiration from his forehead, squinted up at the lean of the eighty-foot spruce he was felling, and then whipped his axe deep into the cut. The smell of pitch was clean in the afternoon air.

Clinging to the rigging of the schooner's furled aft topsail, Beard stared across the water toward San Francisco Presidio, Mission Dolores, and the small village of Yerba Buena. When darkness fell, he concluded, it was altogether possible that he'd simply slip into one of the dinghies trailing from the stern of the *Pride* and row for shore. He'd strike out on his own—a young man, strong and bright, with a good helping of Yankee energy and ingenuity. Having thought the matter through, he decided that his fate lay in becoming rich—yes, a rich man in a new and generally unpopulated land—even if he were required to accept Catholicism as part of the bargain.

The prospect of punishment, should he be caught, was not sufficient to deter him. Vermonters, after all, were not the sort of men to worry overmuch about matters of political convenience. Besides, Beard had a plan—or perhaps it was no more than a wild dream. When the crew put ashore near the San Diego Mission during the northward voyage, one of the good friars had told him of a great range of inland mountains, a place of gigantic canyons and huge trees and green steams of water dashing down from the heights. True, the man hadn't actually been there—but he'd spoken with mestizos who had, and these were men, the good friar asserted, who were known never to speak other than the God's own truth.

The explorers Lewis and Clark had crossed the entire North American continent, and accounts of their venture were widespread, complete with long passages from their journals. The figure of Charbonneau and his Hidatsa-Shoshone wife Sacajawea fascinated Beard. To have seen such land—to have known such a woman, one who embodied the fierceness and the grandeur of the land itself—hell, that was enough to make any seafaring man begin to yearn for a plot of land at the foot of a mountain; yes, and a dusky-skinned woman in his bed.

The life of a seaman was fine enough (most of the time), but the land itself and the red-skinned people who inhabited it . . . Surely this place called *Alta California* was destined to become part of the United States. In any case, the lure was both insane and all but overwhelming. At the present moment, Beard conjectured, the entire, unutterably beautiful, savage *thing* was potentially within his grasp—if only he suffered no failure of nerve. He'd need a horse and a rifle and a quantity of powder and lead. Somewhere beyond the rolling, oak-forested hills to the east of this narrow water. . . .

Drawn by the same lure that took so many Vermont lads, young Beard had eventually gone to sea—but not until after graduation from normal college. It wasn't that he'd actually promised his consumptive, dying mother he'd tend to the education she'd always wanted for him, but rather that he felt as though he'd made such a commitment, even if, in fact, he hadn't. Thus he fulfilled the obligation to his harpsichord-playing matriarch, and she had indeed been proud of him. He and his father had sat there beside her as she quietly, peacefully, made her way from this world into the next.

So it was that after graduation, and after one final summer in the logging woods with his pa, William Beard signed on with a merchant ship, and a single year led to seven—because, after all, though Christie O'Brien promised to wait for *my Billy to come home*, she then proceeded to marry Tom Ebersoll, whose father owned a dairy. The mating was a good one, apparently, for at last count the Ebersolls had spawned three boys and two girls.

As fate would have it, William Beard was shoreside during the latter portion of the War of 1812, and, out of love of country, joined the Vermont Volunteers. He was with Lieutenant Thomas Macdonough, whose small fleet on Lake Champlain defeated the Brits off Plattsburgh, New York—eliminating the threat to Vermont. September eleventh it was, and the year 1814. Fierce though the battle raged, he emerged unscathed—and at the end of the war, he put once again to sea. By this time his father, Bill Senior, was dead, killed by smoke inhalation as he attempted to help a neighbor get his livestock out of a burning barn.

But now Beard felt a powerful urge to go ashore. Was Alta California not a likely place to realize that dreamed-of clearing in the forest, a place where sunlight penetrated gray-green darkness, and multicolored flowers started up from damp earth?

The sea had been wonderful, providing the necessary interval between boyhood and full adulthood. The man named William Beard had indeed emerged. As older hands put it, the sea eventually grew tired of a coon. After that one could no longer joy in those faceless, endless swellings, astonishing storm winds followed by days when the waves were placidly becalmed—from equatorial zones to regions where gaunt ships of ice sailed inexorably past, their ghostly crews unperceived—and deckhands of such craft as *Baltimore Pride* tied scarves about their tingling faces.

Slowly the image of pink-cheeked Christie O'Brien faded. Indeed, he seldom thought of her at all anymore. As to the need for female companionship and full initiation into the mysteries of sexuality, why, the professional ladies of New Orleans, Havana, Buenos Aires, Manila, Honolulu, and Mazatlán had provided him with a fairly thorough education—nor had the tuition at this international, multi-campus institution been excessive. Luckily he'd avoided contracting any of the illnesses common to business dealings with *Señorita La Puta*. He remained hale and hearty, and to the best of his knowledge he'd fathered no children.

Trees . . . such as those giants he'd seen when Captain Fairchild and half his crew took to the dinghies and went ashore in search of tanbark oak, to the south of Pico Blanco. Indeed, he'd seen trees whose size and height were virtually beyond belief, huge columns of dark green foliage supported by boles clad in orange-red bark, serene monsters growing there in the *barrancas*, mysterious and undisturbed. And there in the glade, intrigued by the presence of *Bostons* and yet wary of them, as wary as though the sailors might have been either grizzly bears or cannibals, were bronze-skinned girls ranging in age, or so Beard presumed, from perhaps twelve to eighteen—and all of them bare-breasted, clad in nothing more than short skirts of either deerskin or woven tules. The Indian girls had long black hair, some braided and some not, and sunlight gleamed from their skin.

The seamen began to whoop and holler, setting off toward these children of the wild, even though Captain Fairchild had given no permission, but the girls vanished as if magically. Indeed, it was as if a cave mouth had momentarily yawned open and the Indians had disappeared into it.

Fairchild, sword instinctively drawn, stood there with blade raised high, and he was laughing, laughing. . . .

The old desire had risen in Beard, and no doubt that was why, in his dream, he was returned to the woods of Vermont and the lands first claimed by Samuel de Champlain and subsequently named New Connecticut—and to his boyhood vision of meeting a dark-skinned princess of

the mysterious forest, a vision which covert meetings with
Christie had partially fulfilled.

In any case, the Indian girls were gone—vanished as
certainly as though they'd been nothing more than a
momentary hallucination—and Fairchild's crew went on
about their appointed tasks. But that glade of great redwood
trees and ferns and azaleas just coming into bloom, and
down-slanting beams of sunlight: the place was haunted by
a momentary presence of beauty quite different from the
loveliness of trees. Eden had come alive, and within the
garden were many Eves. *Costanoans*. That's what the Spanish
called these gentle, wild people who inhabited the coastal
forests. Yet another term, as Beard learned later, and one
sometimes used by the Indians themselves, was *Ohlones—the
people who live close by the sea*.

Half a dozen gray and white gulls and a pair of cormorants
drifted over the blue waters of Bahía del San Francisco,
coming close enough to satisfy avian curiosity and, in the
process, to determine that no garbage or unattended food
was lying about, then winging off, soaring on the wind. For
a moment the birds were framed against the sprawling
green form of Mount Tamalpais northward, only to vanish
in a mixture of sunlight and scudding fogbank.

No doubt about it. The air smelled different this day in
1817, deliciously different, and randy March sun was
whispering the kinds of words that turned seasoned sailors
once again into boys with troubles in their breeches. Odors
of pollen, odors of grass, drifted across the bay from rolling,
oak-studded hillsides where new leaves uncoiled in their
own secret fashion from nubs of winter-gray bark. In an area
close by the settlement, bulls bellowed that they might be
allowed to mingle with the cows. Beard could detect faint
notes of guitars, and barely discernible on the air were the
sounds of female voices in song—but was that possible?
Parturition. Mother Earth, bless her gaping thighs, was
once again giving birth to the perpetually recurring, ancient
mystery of springtime.

In the American East the previous summer, just before he'd signed aboard the *Baltimore Pride* for this last cruise, there had as yet been no warm, fair weather to speak of; and some university professors were claiming the whole shift in the natural order of things was due to the explosion of Mount Tambora, with a somewhat greater portion of the sun's radiation reflected back into space because of all the dust in the air. The theory sounded farfetched to Beard, but snow kept falling in spurts, clear on into June.

Whatever Mount Tambora did or didn't cause, the weather continued unpredictable and generally bad until the *Pride* reached anchorage down south, near the San Diego Mission. Now spring was on its way, and no question about it. When one got right down to cases, the present was sure as hell no proper moment for an able-bodied American sailor like William Beard to be at anchor in calm water, and no apparent cure for that malady—or for the other.

Out there, out there somewhere, were young women with closed eyes and parted lips, and such women most certainly needed to be serviced properly. Not to do so was both inhumane and against nature. As part of a little crew that accompanied the brass ashore the previous day, Beard had actually seen the ladies—some of them *Indio* and a few of them *Hidalgo*, the former dressed in featureless brown garments, while the latter wore bright-colored raiment.

The *Pride* had left Baltimore on June 11, 1816, a nearly winterlike day when that city, incidentally, became the first in the nation to use gas for street lighting. Having rounded the Horn, the ship was now some nine months out from Chesapeake Bay. President Madison would have gone into retirement by now, while his former Secretary of State, James Monroe, would already have been inaugurated as the fifth president of the United States. They'd received news of the election when the *Pride* put ashore at Valdivia, shortly before Christmas. Back home, according to reports, the nation was at peace, canals and roads were being constructed, and steamships would soon be plying the Mississippi itself, opening the interior to commerce on a much greater scale.

Yes, and Seaman William Beard was of a mind to put ashore, permanently, amidst alien corn, so to speak, even if there wasn't any corn in sight. He felt no disaffection toward his native country—and indeed he had no real plans to change his national affiliation. It was simply that the general monotony of life aboard ship had finally gotten to him. In short, he lacked adventure.

The last time Cap'n Fairchild got his men stranded, the ship was offshore of Chile's godforsaken Atacama Desert, north of Antofagasta, with no signs of human habitation for miles around, and the sea utterly becalmed. This time, at least, there were ladies, music, and whiskey—all the graces of the *Gente de Razón*, the Californios—except that Fairchild wasn't allowing his men any time ashore, not unless his nibs happened to be along to keep an eye on the lads.

Rumor had it the captain was in the process of dealing for the pelts of sea otters and fur seals—plew that might be sold at a good profit, with consequent bonuses to the crew.

For the past seven years, Beard had been on one sailing craft or another, but now he was inclined to turn landlubber, permanently, in a place where damned few of the natives could even speak English, more likely than not. Some men had a knack for picking up languages, however, and he was one of them. As a boy growing up near Orleans, in northern Vermont, he'd acquired Canuck French from the Canadian families living in the area, and a bit of Coaticook dialect from an old Indian man and his wife who stayed in a cabin near the base of Gore Mountain, an area where the elder Beard and his son sometimes went hunting and where the son subsequently spent one year working in the logging woods. Those, Beard reflected now, had been good times. More to the point, a few weeks ashore in various ports of call such as Vera Cruz and Lima, a year or so earlier, and he'd found he could communicate passably well in Spanish. Such was, at least, a beginning.

For more than a month now, *Pride* had been at anchor inside the nearly land-ringed bay, just a few leagues distant from this bit of civilization called Yerba Buena. Captain Daniel Fairchild and his junior officers, needless to say, spent much time ashore—doubtlessly enjoying the company of those same dark-skinned señoritas and thus rendering proper religious ritual and sacrifice in behalf of the god Priapus, or so the schooner's scuttlebutt ran. Officially, Fairchild was in the process of negotiating with Pablo Vicente de Sola, now that the governor was once again back at this northern outpost.

"Well," Beard mused, "such are the privileges of rank."

For common gobs, however, no such luck and no such privilege prevailed—permission to go ashore had been denied from the first, on grounds that Spanish-Mexican authorities would have to be cajoled, placated, and generally toadied to—for otherwise trading would not be allowed, not even for desperately needed foodstuffs and hempen hawsers, to say nothing of tallow and hides and pelts of various denominations, even though the *Pride* carried trade goods sorely needed in Alta California and not readily available from the outside world.

Official policy forbade trade, except, of course, with Madre Mexico.

The truth of the matter was quite different, for in this remote portion of the Empire of Spain, occasional foreign ships were deemed a necessity—and the *Gente de Razón*, after certain formalities, always found reasons to conduct business. Nonetheless, as Cap'n Fairchild informed his men, Alta California was a closed society, one fearful of outsiders, and of Americans in particular. The province of Upper California, as far as it lay from Mexico City, was seen as particularly vulnerable to probable expansionist schemes— American and Russian and British as well. In the aftermath of the Louisiana Purchase, the aims of Empire America were taken for granted by the Spanish—and would be resisted as a matter of policy against an indefinite future time when necessity might dictate a bloody war for survival.

For the moment, however, Spain had its hands full in attempting to deal with a movement for Mexican independence, a civil war whose issue was still in doubt. In any case, not just the Americans posed a threat to this strange, insular world of Alta California. A few leagues north of the Bahia del San Francisco, the Russians had established an agricultural station and a fort—and further north yet were the British, the monolithic Hudson's Bay Company that sometimes sent trapping expeditions south into the mountains and valleys of California itself.

Governor Pablo Vicente de Sola, presently in Yerba Buena on state business but at other times living the life of a feudal baron near the capital of Monterey, nearly a hundred miles to the south, had reasons for being cautious.

Yet another complication lay in Mexico's strict code of male honor, a code that obtained as fully here in Alta California as elsewhere. Unwelcome attentions paid to *proper* female villagers would certainly result in a hue and cry for revenge—for satisfaction of honor—and possibly for an all-out attack on the *Baltimore Pride*.

Well, no matter. Beard was of a mind to take a calculated risk—a mere half mile of rowing, some California whiskey, a black-haired female with soft breasts and a proper twinkle in her eye—and then the purchase of a horse and saddle as well as a flintlock rifle. Provided only that American coin were found acceptable, by noon tomorrow he'd be on his way southward, beyond the bay and then across mountains that in some ways resembled the hills back in Vermont, to see what the possibilities were in and about the Mission of Santa Cruz and Branciforte Pueblo, about which were said to be living a settlement of deserters and other persons criminally inclined.

If money wouldn't do the job, then he'd be obliged to ride shank's mare, at least until he could solve the problems of international exchange.

When all was said and done, the regimen of forced celibacy on shipboard was unnatural as hell, and Beard was one lad who'd had quite enough of it, thank you.

Petty Officer Coburn would be pacing the deck past sundown, of course, long after everyone else had taken to his quarters—and not out of necessity, but because the Irish lunkhead had a kind of compulsion to be moving about in the night, bad foot and all. In quarters below deck the petty officer's club-footed walk was particularly annoying if a man were trying to catch forty winks—the sound uncannily magnified through ship's timbers, a rhythmic *klump-caa-lump, klump-caa-lump*.

But in terms of the project presently at hand, Seaman Beard concluded, that very sound, Coburn's lame walk, would serve notice as to the proper moment for slipping over the taffrail, duffel and all, hand over hand down a rope ladder and into a trailing dinghy—with as little noise as was humanly possible.

A man had to take his chances if he wanted freedom. He had to be willing to venture beyond the reach of normative order if he wished to realize the full breadth of his own capacities. Civilization, whether administered on shipboard or in a small Vermont town or in the great cities of the world, was the ultimate enemy of the *self*.

It was a matter of those guitars—no, not the guitars, but the voices of women, the lure of dark hair, dark eyes, and doubtless their wonderfully soft flesh—the cries of *las gaviotas* winging across calm waters, as well as those wordless moanings uttered in bed, moanings Beard hoped he would soon recognize as his own. And all of this, and the urgings of spring itself, was bound up inextricably with sirenlike cries of the mysterious land, the continent Lewis and Clark had crossed, the *terra incognita* from whence flowed a presumed Río Buenaventura, draining that wilderness and reaching the Pacific here at Yerba Buena, egress through the Bahía del San Francisco. In such a land, surely, one would be able to venture back into Eden. Was this place, after all, not Paradise? An Eden complete with rattlesnakes and corrupt Spanish priests. . . .

Beard glanced down at the freshly-painted gray deck some eighty feet below, where seamen were engaged in a variety of tasks—from recaulking one of the dinghies to mending sail to working a small forge where I-bolts were being manufactured to replace several that had rusted to the point of being potentially dangerous. He stepped out onto a spar, steadied himself, and with one hand deftly refastened a loose tie-rope.

Then he was back on the ladder and on his way down.

On the beach, just a few hundred yards away, sea lions groaned and snorted, the bulls sluggishly butting heads. The heavy forms of these ungainly beasts were faintly visible among coastal rocks.

William Beard nodded, whistled a dozen notes, and dropped onto the deck of the *Baltimore Pride*.

"Yah-shu, Willy, scrape ye up an' feed yore remains to the crows one o' these days," Bad-Hand John laughed, "unless ye learns to pay heed to caution up thar. Jump about like a fittin' cat, ye do."

Beard shrugged. "Cats may slip at times. New England lads don't. Tend to your caulking, John, or Coburn'll be having your ass for dinner."

Captain Fairchild and his first mate and the four oarsmen of the day returned to the *Baltimore Pride* well before sunset flared its glorious crimson and gold beyond the narrow, rockbound strait that separated the bay from the Pacific Ocean, even as a full, pale amber moon rose above hills to the east, across the water, where fog was already beginning to form.

Beard was one of the hands called upon to winch up three full packs of pelts—sea otters and fur seals. Word had it that barrels of coffee beans and bolts of Yankee cloth would be dispatched ashore the following day. Apparently the final obstacles to trading had been overcome. Fairchild's patience had paid off. With the ship's commanding officer back aboard, call to evening mess came at the usual time. The meal consisted of dumplings and meat, thanks to several sides of beef the Californios had been willing to part with, as a preliminary to actual trading. Thereafter the seamen, singly or by twos and threes, retired to their hammocks below deck. Some of the lads played cards, while others sprawled back against bulkheads and talked about those pieces of land they intended to buy when the cruise was over—or about true loves left behind and no doubt still faithfully awaiting their return—or about certain professional ladies in New Orleans or Río or San Salvador. One or two fellows grumbled about Fairchild's prohibition against going ashore unattended, and others theorized as to the cause of the present extended stay and the probability of receiving official permission to take on cargo and so to be out upon the wind-whipped sea once again, headed north.

One old salt began to play his harmonica, several smoked pipes full of coarse South American tobacco, and Bad-Hand Johnny told a new version of that story of how, as a boy, he accidentally stowed away on a Dutch East Indiaman tied up in Stockholm, bound for Richmond, Virginia, and from thence south to various ports of call in the Caribbean and on to Dutch Guiana. Johnny claimed he'd been hired to assist in loading cargo for a Stockholm dry-goods merchant, in the performance of which task he'd subsequently fallen asleep in the hold and hadn't awakened until the craft was a dozen miles out of harbor. Upon reaching Virginia, however, the Dutch East Indiaman was officially detained, and Bad-Hand John deserted and signed on with a Yankee whaling craft—and so had learned English in the process.

A sailor named Owens professed not to believe John's story—on the grounds that John had self-evidently never learned English at all.

Beard closed his eyes and attempted to get an hour's sleep. When the others eventually quieted down, his necessaries already stowed in his duffel bag, he'd be on his way. Once above deck, avoiding both Coburn and those who stood watch, he'd begin his solitary venture ashore. With the hum of male voices and strangely melancholic notes of a harmonica swirling around him, Beard dozed off. . . .

A dusky, faintly perfumed señorita clung to him as the two of them stood together outside a cantina. Her body was warm against his. Then she laughed, a sound almost like sea

*gulls crying, and tilted her face toward his. He leaned over
to kiss her, pressing his mouth against hers, insinuating his
tongue between faintly resisting lips, and at the same time
his hands went down to cup the pliant fullness of her
derriere. Then a voice rang out, a harsh, authoritative male
voice, a challenging cluster of words in rapid Spanish—
lingo he only half understood. A horse pistol was drawn.
There was no time to dodge, no time to get out of the
way. . . . Instantly a white flare of gunpowder blossomed
toward him. He waited for the crushing, penetrating force of
lead, a force that would in all likelihood end his life. . . .*

Waves slapping against the ship's wooden hull, a regular,
half-heard sound—rhythmic . . . A candle lamp on the far
bulkhead guttered, on the verge of going out. A rat danced
its way along an overhead timber. Men snored loudly.
Beard checked the coins in his pockets, thrust his somewhat
awkward pepperbox pistol under his belt, slipped out of his
hammock, shouldered his gear, and made his way above
deck. He listened for Coburn's uneven gait, but that sound
was not at the moment evident in the close warm darkness.
Lamps were burning in the captain's quarters, however,
and indeed muted voices were audible—Fairchild and his
brass-button underlings were doubtless engaged in swilling
rum, while above, in the foremast crow's nest, the first
watch apparently stirred about—inasmuch as the lantern
was swaying to and fro.

Beard glanced shoreward but could see nothing. The
ubiquitous fogs of this area had rolled in for the night, and
whatever lights might be burning among the clustered
small buildings of the village were not visible. The air, he
noted, smelled different than usual—saltier, heavier, more
unsettled. For a few moments he entertained second
thoughts as to the wisdom of what he'd schemed. Potential
complications were significant, and the reward was far from
certain. If he were apprehended, there'd be ten lashes and
a fine to boot. The specter of potential punishment was now
beginning to weigh heavily in his assessment of the matter

at hand. In another six months, after all, he'd be back in Maryland, at the *Pride*'s home port. With his pay in hand, that would be time sufficient to strike out for the wilderness. . . .

Petty Officer Coburn exited from the captain's quarters, gait more uneven than usual, and *klump-caa-lumped* his way to the guardrail, there fumbling with his breeches and pissing overboard into thick, slow-moving fog. That business tended to, Coburn shouted aloft to the man in the crow's nest, received a brisk *Yo, sir!* in return, and then clumped his way back to Fairchild's quarters.

Beard was on the verge of returning below deck when impulse took him, and, moving with the agility of a cat, he slipped aft, crouching, past the cabin and onto the taffrail. In an instant he was across and on his way down a cord ladder to the captain's special dinghy below. Should anyone shine a lantern over the rail, of course, the missing rowboat would be evident—even with this thick fog. But once Bill Beard was overboard, worry was beside the point, and he loosened the craft's line and began to row slowly toward the blur of a full moon that was well up into the sky, evident through the fog or, a moment later, swallowed utterly. Silver gleamed from undulating waves as moonlight suffused the mist, and after a few minutes he found his rhythm and stroked confidently ahead in the direction in which he presumed land to lie.

What lies ahead of me? God save my Yankee soul, I haven't the faintest idea. . . .

2

Raymondo Quixote

Should he lose his nerve and decide to return a few hours hence, Beard reflected, it would be no simple matter—since the local fogs tended to blanket everything from midnight until well into the morning hours, burning off under full sunlight of midday. Even the present problem of finding his way to the coastline after dark would be difficult enough, while retracing that same watery route without even the aid of a lantern; yes, and actually finding the *Baltimore Pride* somewhere in the midst of the bay's running mists, why, that was a different kettle of fish. Flounders, most likely.

Hell, Beard thought, just possibly this Vermont Yankee can't come back at all, not even if he changes his fool mind. I've set out to burn my bridges, so I've got to be pretty damned certain of what I'm doing. But am I? Jesus Christ, maybe I've done little more than to give in to a whim—I'm acting the part of a madman . . . or an adolescent.

Christie, my own true love, are you waiting for me there ashore? How'd you get to Alta California, Christie, and did you bring that raft of younguns with you? Hell no you're not here—you're in Tom Ebersoll's bed, with your tail in the air. In all likelihood you're fat, stupid, happy, and pregnant again. . . .

16

Then the dinghy's keel slipped over mud. William Beard dragged the craft onto the littoral, looped a tie rope around a stump half buried in silt, and made his way up onto a bank where, as he recalled from his previous trip ashore, numerous yellow bush lupines were in bloom. He stowed his gear, pistol and all, and walked briskly through moon-suffused mists toward the main portion of the village of Yerba Buena.

Once inside a candlelit cantina, Beard relaxed to the music of a guitar that was being played by a señorita perched provocatively on a stool and dressed all in red, a young lady who might have been anywhere from fifteen to thirty, one who appeared to be half angel and half whore, a virtual Mary Magdalene if ever he'd seen one. He watched the guitar player, winked at her several times, indulged himself in a series of shots of whiskey—and soon found himself somewhat less than fully capable of maintaining his balance without holding tightly to the bar.

The young woman in red, to speak plainly, was no Christie O'Brien—and possibly that was all to the good.

Whatever the nature of the attraction, he realized, it was folly to stay too long. To pass out drunk and to be discovered in that condition come morning would virtually guarantee his being apprehended and returned to the *Pride*. No, he resolved, he'd walk southward, keeping more or less to the shore of the bay, and survive as best he could. Perhaps a three days' journey, perhaps four, would bring him to the pueblo of San José de Guadalupe, and once there, he hoped, he'd be able to purchase the things he needed, a horse foremost among them, and so continue toward Branciaforte, near Santa Cruz—a village from which the *Baltimore Pride* had been turned away, at the same time being directed northward to Yerba Buena, where Governor Sola was said to be visiting, and so it had been.

Still, the voluptuous young woman in the red dress was indeed a sight for sore eyes, however untouchable she might be for the likes of a Vermonter named Billy Beard, newly deserted from an American merchant vessel. But a man was free, after all, to fantasize all sorts of things, free to imagine the wild, the unihibited cries such a dark-haired beauty might make during an act of lust. Might she not even howl like the coyotes one could hear at night from shipboard? Or squeal and giggle like a teenaged girl who'd decided to sample her father's jug of hard cider?

Perhaps another drink or two, then, and he'd actually begin to lay plans for enjoying the favors of this dark-haired beauty in red, this *crimson rose of California*, before the night was finished. . . .

"Good stuff, good stuff!" Beard nodded to a large, surly-looking individual seated beside him. The Californio, possibly full-blooded Indian from appearances—a graduate, then, of one of the Spanish missions—was wearing a clay-colored sombrero, perhaps the largest hat the Vermonter had ever seen. The Indio stared mournfully and directly into an empty mug before him. His face, Beard thought, strangely resembled a sweet potato.

"*Sí, no, sí—Yengee stupido bastardo*, huh? Fugga-you, Yengee. Go back you *buque mercante. Tengo sed*. . . ."

Beard shrugged, grinned, feigned ignorance of *Español*.

"I don't guess you're the friendliest fella I ever met, Big Hat," Beard replied. "Don't even know English, eh? Just a few words? Guess I can say pretty much whatever I want to, then, as long as I keep showing my teeth. . . ."

The potato head came around, eyes deep-set, uneven teeth rotting away—the features themselves all but diabolic.

"Know Yenglish. Fugga-fugga, Boston Yengee. *Conprende?*"

"Appreciate your concern, mate, I really do—but that ostrich to which I made reference, or possibly it was a giraffe, it had six legs and smelled like a slaughterhouse on the Fourth o'July, and that's a fact. Get right down to it, *El Sombrero Grande*, I figure you've been humping sheep for so long that you don't know anything else and are thus blameless in the matter and therefore not responsible for the commission of earthly sin original. How stands the union, big fella? I wonder if you might be so kind as to give me a short disquisition on the concept of virtue through endurance, as presented in Sam Johnson's little book, *Rasselas?*"

"*Que quiere decir eso?* Fugga-you, Boston Yengee. Buy Pedro drink, *por favor? Una tequila?*"

Beard laughed. Certain phrases, he'd long since concluded, were virtually universal. He nodded to the barkeep, pointed to his companion's empty shot glass and his own as well, and then made a clucking sound with his tongue—by way of punctuation. The barkeep waited until Beard had put down some American coins, and then he sauntered forward, flask in hand.

The ritual of drinking together resolved the problem of incipient hostility. Between shots of well-diluted tequila, Beard admired the full breasts of the red-clad Indian woman who played guitar so skillfully and sang sad songs about love: man and woman separated by fate and high winds . . . a lonely woman whose lover was in a stockade, doomed to be hung . . . lovers whose marriage was postponed because the bridegroom had been impressed into the Leather Jackets and forced to fight against wild Indians beyond Río Sur, where the mountains drop off precipitously to a stormy ocean *(oceano tormento)* . . . a woman whose lover was lost when his sailing vessel sank on its way back from Spain. All in all, the selections were both charming and melancholy—and precisely right, as Beard gazed upon his imagined scarlet-clad vessel of desire, a vessel from which no doubt he was doomed never to drink.

For a moment he could almost feel her in his arms— the aroma of her—candlelight glinting from her even white teeth—his hand slipping down inside her bodice. . . .

Beard shook his head, rose, excused himself, and staggered through a side door and outside to a latrine area. Relieving himself, he gazed up at the blurred roundness of the moon, pale silver through mists, and attempted to will his wits back to clarity, though without great success. He took a lungful of damp air, straightened his shoulders, buttoned his breeches, and valiantly started back to the cantina.

The night had grown preternaturally quiet. Crickets and tree frogs, singing happily just a few minutes before, were now silent. Then dogs in the village nearby began to howl, and at a greater distance coyotes broke into frenzied yapping. Then they, too, were still.

For whatever reasons, the *pulcra musica* had left off playing her guitar, and Beard felt a chill run along his spine. He started to walk back to the cantina but suddenly found myself face to face with none other than Petty Officer Coburn and four hands from the *Baltimore Pride*.

"You're under ship's arrest, Seaman Beard," Coburn said, his voice utterly monotone. "You may be charged with the high crime of desertion, you Vermont lunkhead. At the very least there's the matter of theft of the captain's dinghy, oars, lines, and so forth. . . . Matters will go better for you if you offer no resistance. Your generally good record will be taken into account, naturally."

At precisely that moment Beard's Indio drinking partner pushed through, muttering incoherently and appearing for all the world as though his stomach contents might erupt through his mouth at any instant. As a result, Coburn's lackey, who'd been directed to lay fast to Beard, hesitated—just long enough for Beard to give *Sombrero Grande* a brisk push, sending the heavyset individual lurching into Coburn himself, who staggered backward, cursing.

Big Hat, feeling himself practiced upon, took a wild swing at Coburn. The petty officer slipped away from the punch, drew his fleet pistol, and leveled the weapon at the large Indio.

Then came a much greater push. The earth heaved beneath their feet, heaved again, and then vibrated for perhaps thirty seconds, and everyone present found himself on hands and knees as terra firma demonstrated its inherently infirm nature.

The sounds of timbers cracking, and then the sod roof

of the cantina collapsed, and a portion of one bearing wall came down. Dust boiled into the darkness, and those within the partially collapsed building began to cry out.

William Beard turned, bolted away. Suddenly quite sober, he dashed into the misty dark. He could hear angry shouts behind him, Coburn's voice filling the night with curses. Hardly certain which way he was heading, Beard raced along the roadway where he'd ambled in happy anticipation, moving in the opposite direction, only a couple of hours earlier. When another, lesser temblor rattled through the earth, he veered, fighting his way through a thicket of bush lupines and willows.

In the fog-enhanced gloom, he ran into something heavy, bounced off, fell backward, and gasped for breath. A grunting sound, followed by deep-throated bellowing—these sounds and the sloshing of hooves stamping about in muck. . . .

A bull lowed amorously, no doubt one of those he'd heard from the ship.

Beard sucked for breath, rose to his feet, and rubbed at his face.

"Bastards, bastards—I've broke my gawddamned nose, sure as hell. . . ."

Then he moved away from the startled longhorn, made mental corrections for a detour, and plunged toward what he hoped would be the approximate area where he'd landed the captain's dinghy—if the earthquake hadn't caused the whole beach area to slip off into the waters of the bay.

Was it possible that Coburn had already discovered the craft, set a guard?

Damn the fog!

Have to get to my duffel—helpless without it—the bastards aren't taking me aboard the Pride *again, no by Christ's teeth and toenails, and there's no way this Vermont coon's going to have his back whipped raw and then be obliged to rot for a month or so in Fairchild's goddamned brig. . . . Why in hell did I let myself get soused? Stupido bastardo, just like Big Hat said. I should have made tracks, should have put as much distance behind me as possible. . . .*

He slipped in thick mire, a swampy area. But now, at least, he knew where he was.

Already there were torches coming down the hill, perhaps a quarter of a mile behind—Coburn and his men, hopefully no one else, no full posse. . . . With luck the boys would run afoul of a somewhat bad-tempered bull, one who'd been disturbed quite enough for one night, thank you.

Beard sprinted downslope, came to the mud and sand beach and quickly found his duffel, pulled it open, withdrew the pepperbox pistol. He crouched there, waited. The lead torch, he noted, moved irregularly—*Coburn himself, that limping banty rooster!* Beard set his pistol's hammer and said a short prayer to a presumed God of Dry Powder.

Then noise and the odor of gun smoke. Petty Officer Coburn, no more than a hundred feet away at this instant and faintly visible by torchlight, was yelling at the top of his lungs, at the same time clutching his forearm.

Now it's a hanging offense, Willy Beard the philosopher.

Fog lay over the water, and Beard was obliged to feel his way forward to the beach itself. Several shots came in answer, but he was confident his pursuers wouldn't immediately risk an attempt to rush him. Within moments he was into the dinghy, duffel and all, and was rowing away from shore—at least, he presumed that's what he was doing—for fog hung unbelievably thick, and not even the moon's rays could pierce it. Beard gauged directions, realized the near futility of worrying the matter, set himself, and strained at the oars. With more luck than anyone had a right to claim, he'd make it across to the eastern limit of this bay that was nearly surrounded by hills.

He felt his gorge begin to rise, and within moments, beyond the mind's capacity to control the body's imperatives, he heaved painfully all over his clothing—a stew of half-digested beef and biscuit, whiskey, tequila, and bile.

Sucking for air, he cursed himself for his unbelievable folly. He cleared his throat and spat into darkness.

Fog still hung over the water the following morning, a leaden blanket of mist so heavy he couldn't even detect the direction of the sun. Rather than attempt to continue his trans-bay voyage, William Beard removed his outer clothing, used the shirt as a scrub cloth, and swabbed out the dinghy. Then he scrubbed both breeches and shirt, wringing them as dry as possible, and pulled them back on.

For all he knew, he might be rowing directly toward the *Baltimore Pride*—indeed, his voyage might well have described a circle and hence have brought him back to within a stone's throw of Yerba Buena itself. Unfortunately, all was mere supposition—he had no way of knowing and no way of finding out. Exhausted, he lay down in the keel and slept—trusted to relatively placid waters and occasional bursts of wind. Some force greater than his own had taken charge—call it Fate, call it God. Whatever it was, the motion of the dinghy was almost like that of a child's cradle, the sort one hung from a cherry bough on a Saturday afternoon in July. As uncomfortable as he was, sleep called him down within a matter of minutes.

Sunlight awoke him once again, but for a time he lay there confused, uncertain how long he might have slept or why he wasn't in his hammock on shipboard. He squinted into the brilliance, shielded his eyes. A trace of blue sky appeared directly overhead.

A pelican, its head cocked to one side, stared down. The large, ungainly, yellow-gray bird was perched on the very prow of the dinghy—and was slowly fanning its great wings.

"Good afternoon, bilge belly," Beard managed. "Afraid I've got nothing to offer—not so much as a damned sardine. The truth is, my fine feather bucket, I'm hungry as hell myself. I'll give you some advice, though. Hear me now. Avoid strong drink, friend. Old Scratch Diabolo invented the brew."

The pelican nodded wisely.

For his own part, Beard sat up, pulled himself onto the seat, and grinned.

"So tell me, pouch mouth, which way's east? Southeast will do, as a matter of fact. . . ."

The big bird launched itself forward, barely clearing the man's head, and went flapping off into a wall of shining mist.

Beard slipped the oars into the locks, dipped blades into the water, and spun the craft about. From the position of a nearly midday sun, he deduced which way to head. He drew on the oars, and the dinghy slid forward through a series of gentle swells. Within a matter of minutes, he'd actually emerged from a dissipating fog bank. Turning, the Yankee smiled to see the familiar outline of those big green eastward hills directly ahead, with shore itself lying no more than perhaps half a mile off.

Beard entertained a distinct notion that one life had fallen away behind him, and another lay ahead. The present moment signaled the passage.

Three days later, traveling afoot, he approached a cluster of adobe buildings surrounded by cultivated fields and pasture lands at the head of a low, narrow plain rising from the *bahía* to the mountains that rose eastward. He waved to various brown-skinned workers as he approached the complex, some engaged in repairing a tumbled-down— collapsed, Beard supposed, due to the recent earthquake. He called out greetings in Spanish, and ultimately strode through the gateway and into the neatly laid out courtyard. Here he addressed himself to the good friars at the Mission Santa Clara de Guadalupe, essentially throwing himself upon their Christian mercy, at the same time informing them that his name was Benjamin Barrington. The priests listened attentively to his not altogether correct Spanish, nodded wisely, sat him down at a table whereon was a ceramic plate heaped with cold meats, flour cakes, and beans, as well as a pitcher of goat's milk. While he ate his solitary meal, the friars arranged for an audience with Padre Orontes, the mission's director and, Beard gathered, its ranking candidate for sainthood.

When, as *Señor Barrington*, he was presented to the holy man, Orontes nodded and then asked a series of questions concerning the circumstances of Beard's departure from his former occupation.

"Yes, Father, I'm an American, though I've been employed for several years now as ship's carpenter aboard the *H.M.S. Dover*, presently captained by John Singleton of Leeds. Several of us were sent ashore to secure a quantity of spirit gum, but unfortunately our small craft was swamped in the waves as we approached land, and my four mates drowned. I alone survived—because the Almighty put it into my head to hang onto the keel of our capsized craft. The others attempted to swim beachward and were overwhelmed by the sea. As fate would have it, then, I was washed ashore safe and sound. . . ."

The corpulent Orontes' shifted in his chair and adjusted his waist cord. His voice was deep and pleasant, like rhubarb pie. The face was round and beardless, the eyes brown and intense. Orontes general expression suggested boredom—or the desire to get on to other matters.

"And when did this happen, *por favor?*"

"Nearly a month ago, Father. You see, a rainstorm came on, one with extremely high winds—and I was obliged to work my way inland in order to find shelter. Doubtless Captain Singleton sent a search party as soon as the weather calmed down, but I was unfortunate enough to—"

"*Señor Barrington*, is it? *Sí, por cierto*, I recall that storm—it nearly took away our roof! *Bien*, how is it an American should be serving aboard a British vessel?"

Orontes touched the tips of his fingers to his lips.

"Commandeered, Father. We were at port of call in the Sandwich Islands, and I drank a bit too much grog. When I awoke, the Brits had me aboard their blarsted craft. Oh, I was outraged at first, but after a time I got to liking it."

"You came from far south of Monterey, then? *Hay montañas*—but you found your way across? Well, *Señor Barrington*, what do you wish of me? Would you care to be given transport to Yerba Buena? I understand a Yankee trading vessel is presently anchored there. Perhaps the captain would be willing to take you on, and thus you would be able to make your way back to Boston or *Neuva York*."

"No," Beard replied. "With the Father's permission, I'd like to stay here, in this land—in California. I have no wish to go home again. Perhaps you have carpentry work? That's what I'm best at and what I was trained to do. I'm also skilled with a falling axe and an adze."

"Possibly, possibly. You appear to be strong in the arms and back. We will see. You are not fleeing from the law? I have contacts with Monterey, you know. . . . For right now, however, perhaps we can use you in the *caballeriza*. Do you have a gift for horses as well as for fabricating things *a de madera*? If that is so, then we can provide you with a way to earn your room and board, at the very least. The man who works there now is very lazy, a *paseante*. Perhaps you'll exercise a good influence over him. Otherwise I will have to have him beaten one of these days. Indio, you see, an Ohlone. This one wishes to be a scholar, *por Dios!*"

With a somewhat malevolent wink, Father Orontes began to chuckle and to nod his head, having made, perhaps, a small jest that he presumed his American guest did not fully understand.

Except that Beard did comprehend, just as he had come to realize that this Fray Orontes was a man with very few principles—one who loved power for its own sake. In all likelihood, he had his way with the Indian women there at the mission, and possibly with the young boys as well. . . .

Once escorted to the stables, Beard was introduced to a small, intense man by the name of Raymondo Olivo, an Ohlone long since converted to Catholicism, at least so far as appearances were concerned, one whom the good fathers had captured when he was but ten years old.

Render unto me the little children.

The two men shook hands, and, in the time-honored way of males, made quick estimate of the other's essential nature and, of course, probable areas of strength and weakness.

Olivo winked and muttered, in English, something about Augean Stables. The Yankee nodded, not at first realizing an allusion had been made to Greek mythology. Then he caught the significance of the remark—a memory trace, perhaps, of something he'd first read in the fifth or sixth grade in a small, drafty Vermont schoolroom and had more recently attended to at the normal college in Montpelier.

"Hercules," Beard allowed, "was at a disadvantage. There are two of us."

"True, true enough. Yet these stables are much larger. After all, Señor Benjamin Barrington, these stables, they belong to the King of Spain, the most powerful man in all the world."

"I'd suppose they belonged to the Pope . . ." Beard shrugged.

"The Pope and the King—are they not one and the same? What do I know? After all, I am but an Indian."

Olivo was, as one of the priests quickly pointed out, knowledgeable in both Spanish and English, as well as the Costanoan dialects—a man with a passion for learning. He was presumed to have read nearly every book in the mission.

"It is sad, *muy triste*," the priest said, "such a passion for knowledge—and yet merely an Indio."

When the friar had left, hands deftly inserted into the sleeves of a brown serge robe, Olivo and Beard nodded, and Raymondo gestured as if to indicate that the Celestial Bossman had made things as they were, and hence the futility of attempting to change Divine Order. He handed the American a manure fork.

"For the King of Spain?" Beard asked.

"*Sí*, yes *amigo*, for someone like that we do this job.

Perhaps next month we will discover that we are working for the Emperor of Mexico. Who can be sure? Perhaps after that we shall labor for the Emperor of Alta California. I do not know. This way, this way, Benjamin . . ."

"Call me *Bill*—it's, well, you might say it's short for Benjamin. Anyhow, Bill's what my friends call me, and I'm used to it."

Olivo looked puzzled.

"*Bill? Guillermo*, is it not? *William?* I knew one other American. He was also strange. He came south from Astoria with a group of British trappers. He was a blacksmith and showed me the proper way to shoe a horse. A crazy man named Samson Flowers. Is it possible you know him, Señor Barrington?"

"And you—you call yourself *Raymondo* or just plain *Ray*? You must be aware that the United States is a large country—even larger than Mexico. It isn't likely that I would know this. . . . Flowers."

Olivo winked again.

"Of course, of course. And yes, I call myself something like that."

"My pap," Beard confided, "he always said it was permissible to call a man anything but *Late for Chow*."

Olivo frowned for a moment, rapped his manure fork against the gateway to one of the stalls, and then smiled, nodded.

"'Get to the back of the boat,' Noah stated sternly. Maybe you and I, *amigo*, we will get along," he said.

Beard moved into Olivo's bachelor quarters—one of the several straw and adobe huts whose rear walls abutted an adobe granary which served the mission and its population of brown-frocked friars, half a dozen Leather Jacket soldiers, and perhaps three hundred more-or-less civilized Indians, primarily Ohlones but a few of them Miwoks and Pomos from an indeterminate region to the north of the Bahía del San Francisco.

The granary wall, Beard noted, had a crack of recent

vintage running through it, edges fresh and still crumbling, descending irregularly from left to right. An older but otherwise similar crack separated the adobe bricks on a nearly vertical plane.

"Earthquakes are common in this part of the world, or so I gather," Bill Beard remarked. "The jolt three days ago—that what cracked the wall?"

Olivo nodded.

"*Temblor de tierra?* A big tree must have come down in the Sierra Santa Cruz. The earth shakes when a giant *madera roja* loses its strength and falls. The trees back in the *barrancas*, they are excessively large, Señor Barrington."

Beard studied Olivo.

"You pulling my Yankee leg?"

"*Tomarle el pelo?* No, no. I was told this when I was a child—it is something my people believe, the Ohlones. There are places around here where very large trees grow—perhaps the largest trees in the world."

Beard took in this bit of information with a few grains of salt, nodded, and stared once more at the cracks in the granary wall.

Olivo carved off portions of dried beef and added these to a stew of vegetables left over from the previous evening's meal. While the not-altogether-appetizing conglomeration in a small black kettle was heating over an open fire just outside the entryway, Olivo nodded and produced a tallow-impregnated leather flask of red wine of no particular vintage—a mixture thick, sour, and ropy at the same time. After a long day of working in the stables, however, the vino was welcomed. Each man took a pull from the flask, and then they settled down, relaxed, waiting for the stew to simmer.

"All we need now is a couple of bitches," Beard grinned.

"*Perras o señoritas?*"

"*Señoritas, desde . . .desde luego.*"

Raymondo Olivo nodded.

"Most of the time the padres, they treat us well

enough," he remarked. "And yet, do you understand, *Don Bill*, whether they allow us to have women or not, we are slaves—no, we are like the serfs in medieval times in Europe. It is here as it must have been in Westphalia or the north of Italy or in *España* itself. You are surprised that I know of these things? The good friars, they let me read, you see—yes, at such times as I have nothing else to do. In some way the brown robes are actually proud of me— perhaps as one would be proud of a talking dog, except for Father Orontes, who doesn't like me at all. I think he wishes young Tereza to visit him in his chamber, but she is an innocent, and so she prefers me—except that she doesn't yet know what it truly is to prefer a man. Perhaps one day I will run away with Tereza, but only if she will agree to leave her mother here at the mission. *Hombre!* Where you come from, Guillermo, did you leave a woman behind? You are married, perhaps?"

Beard thought momentarily of Christie O'Brien but then shook his head.

"No," he replied, "I'm afraid I'm a randy bachelor."

Olivo drank a bit more wine, passed the flask to the man from Vermont, and then stood up.

"The friars," he said, "they're simple souls, actually, and not altogether bad. Look, Señor Guillermo Barrington, what I have here. I do not own much, but to me this page-worn old book is most precious. . . ."

3

The Goodness of Padre Orontes

From beneath his straw pallet, Olivo produced a thick volume entitled *Don Quixote*, written by Miguel Cervantes.

"The God-men pay me a little," Olivo continued. "Truly, they are the agents of Jesus. For six months I save what I can—then I buy the book from a trader with whom I have become friendly. I have no idea where he got it—maybe he stole it. In any case, the book came all the way from Spain. It was printed in a city called Seville—that's what the imprint says. One day, Guillermo, I will have many books—maybe a whole shelf full of books. I tell you it is so. I have learned my lessons well."

Beard took the volume from Olivo's hand, turned the pages, nodded.

The Californio priests, he'd come to realize, did an amazingly thorough job. They removed Indian children from their villages and fed them and clothed them and in some cases taught them to read and write, at the same time proceeding to erase the last vestiges of native awareness, whatever kind of awareness the Ohlone way might have been. Customs, family, religion, spiritual experience—all were stripped. Such a transformation could only be deemed

31

astounding. Take for instance, as the drunken Pedro at
Yerba Buena—that was one result, unfortunately. Once
freed from mission life, Pedro was without identity, without
direction.

"Well, this Cervantes guy," Beard scowled, playing the
country bumpkin part that had served him well on the
Pride, "he couldn't write English very good. Hell, Raymondo, his spelling's lots worse than mine even."

"*Sí, sí, esta bien*, Cervantes, he has no trouble spelling
the words in *Español*. He writes in pure Castillian."

Beard scratched the side of his nose and then ran his
fingers over his mustache.

"You telling me this fellow's a damned foreigner?"

"No, no. You are the foreigner, Benjamin Guillermo.
Very dense, very dense."

"Well, Raymondo, then explain. This book, what's she
about?"

Beard could see that Olivo had been hoping the
question might be asked.

"Don Quixote, he undertakes a quest in behalf of
Dulcinea del Toboso—and so he attacks the windmills, he
attacks the sheep, he attacks many things. Once he even
goes into a cage with a lion."

"Any fella who'd do that for a woman can't be very
bright." Beard grinned. "I mean, what's in it for him? Does
he get little Tereza, or what?"

Raymondo Olivo stood up, strode across the room to
the entryway, and then turned around.

"Bill is short for Benjamin—then what is Barrington
short for? If we are to be friends, señor, it is only right for
you to tell me your true name. Otherwise I must call you
Sancho. I will be Raymondo Quixote, and you will be
Sancho Panza the Boston Man."

"I guess you've got a point," Beard admitted. "Give me
another drink from the wine flask, *el pellejo*, and perhaps
that will help me to remember."

Olivo studied the American as he drank.

"Well?" he persisted.

"Beard—just like this thing on my face. William Beard

of Vermont, at your service. My pa raised me up to be a log cutter, but my mom insisted that I take up school-teaching. So I went to normal college, and after I graduated, I slipped tether and made for the sea."

"*Normal* college? I don't understand—what sort of place is that?"

"Teaches teachers how to teach, that's all—instead of studying the Bible."

Raymondo nodded three times.

"The sea? The sea, it is very big and very lonely. Sometimes I have met such men, the ones from the sailing ships, and it seems to me always they are very sad—as though they've lost something far out on the great waters of the ocean. Perhaps they've lost their souls, *las ánimas*."

"And then again," Beard replied, "maybe that isn't the reason at all."

"In any case, the cutting of logs, that is better I think. *El leñador*, is it not so? You want logs to cut, William Beard? I could show you such trees that you would not otherwise believe. *Ad por desgracia*, they do not grow close to the pueblo and the mission. No, a few of these great tree people live on the other side of the mountains, but there are many more in the Santa Cruz Range, close by the sea. Later on you can teach children how to read and write, if you wish."

"Redwoods?" Beard asked, one eyebrow rising slightly. "The giants I've been hearing about? In Vermont the folks'd call the whole thing a fish story. The truth is, though, I've seen a few of them—little things, back in from the coast, south of Monterey."

Vividly Beard recalled the huge columnlike orange-red boles he'd seen during Fairchild's tanbark venture, and so he knew Olivo spoke the truth. Still, there was little reason to admit to knowledge—not while he could use ignorance as a pretense for pulling Raymondo's leg a bit.

"*Pez?* You do not believe me, Señor Barring—Beard? I tell you these trees are very big, *muy grande*."

Beard pretended to mull the report. He pursed his lips

and squinted in what he presumed to be properly skeptical fashion.

"Let's say a man cut one down. The stump—what would it measure across the top?"

"The biggest of the trees?"

"Sure. Why not? The biggest damned tree you know of." Olivo grinned.

"No one could cut down such a tree, Señor Bill."

"Sure, sure, I know. Like you say, Raymondo, these are *big trees* we're talking about. But just say someone did—how wide would that stump be? Four feet? Five feet?"

Olivo squinted, nodded his head.

"I tell you, but you do not believe me. Perhaps one day we should ride over the mountains behind the mission. In Moraga Canyon they grow—not the greatest, but big, very big. Such a stump, it would be ten feet maybe, fifteen feet. Maybe more even."

"A thousand years in Purgatory for telling such tales, Ray old friend. I mean—ten feet I could believe. But fifteen?"

"At least fifteen," Olivo insisted. "Perhaps even twenty. There is no Purgatory for telling the truth—but only for failing to believe it."

The American pulled at his chin whiskers and nodded.

"Purgatory, eh? What's the Big Guy make you do once you're there? We Protestants, you understand, we don't have such a place. Protestants are far more civilized than Catholics."

Olivo clucked his tongue.

"For you people, life itself is Purgatory. For Catholics also. But my people, the Ohlones I mean, we listen to Tio Coyote. He tells us very fine stories indeed. If we will not believe him, he holds his breath until he dies. Then he comes back to life. He's very good at resurrection. Twenty feet and more, Señor Beard, just as I have said all along."

The days of California springtime drifted by, a blending of occasional rain showers interspersed with intervals of brilliant sunlight, though often enough the sun didn't actually burn its way through morning mists until morning was halfway toward noon. Grapevines in well-ordered rows, at first gnarled, knobby-looking fists of apparent deadwood, were now laden luxuriantly with leaves and blossom clusters of what would be purple grapes, or so Raymondo insisted, by the end of the long California summer. Fields of wheat and corn were also thriving, and longhorned cattle ambled from one place to another pretty much as they chose, often with an eye toward making incursions into the grain or melon fields.

The land, Beard observed, was unbelievably rich. In colder, less fecund Vermont, gardens had to be tended, nursed, protected. But here—here all a man had to do was drop seeds upon the ground and then, to exaggerate just a bit, get out of the way.

Olivo insisted the previous summer had been both cooler and rainier than usual, while the past winter had several times witnessed snowfall high up on the mountains to the east of the mission, as well as on Tamalpais, to the north. Indeed, he maintained that during most years no rain at all fell during the interval from May through September. Possibly then, William Beard surmised, the great explosion of Mount Tambora had indeed wrought its effect even in Alta California. Whatever the case concerning that geologic prodigy, however, the weather seemed now of a mind to return to normal.

The *Baltimore Pride* had long since set sail, presumed bound for northern waters and then on to Kamchatka and thereafter south to the Philippine Islands; with Captain Fairchild and his crew, went the threat of Beard's being apprehended and taken back aboard the craft which he'd left under such irregular circumstances.

The friendship between Olivo and Beard strengthened quickly—and indeed surprised both men by its inevitability, its rightness. However different from the other each had in the beginning presumed himself to be, commonalities of interest surfaced again and again. The two men in fact began to lay plans to leave Santa Clara de Guadalupe

and to make their way southward to Monterey—or better
yet, to Santa Cruz, where the civic pueblo of Branciforte
was said to stand but a mile distant from the mission itself,
the pueblo an institution whose original purpose, according
to Raymondo, had been military defense, housing Leather
Jacket soldiers, and warehousing stores of arms, gunpowder, and other military necessities—but a place that had
subsequently attracted a civilian population of deserters
from ships of various nations, as well as those Mexican-
Spanish soldiers and sailors who preferred to receive their
discharges a goodly distance from home. After a time,
religious authority no longer prevailed at all in Branciforte,
and close about the pueblo sprang up a considerable village
of outcasts, no-goods, vagabonds, and either actual or
would-be criminals.

In this village, Raymondo and Bill Beard concluded,
they might blend in fairly well—and ultimately they might
find the assistance necessary to run the hypothetical ranch
of which the would-be partners dreamed—*El Rancho
Grande*. Perhaps they'd ultimately make petition to the
government for title to a land grant, to Mexico itself, should
the present and protracted revolution prove ultimately
successful, though Olivo was of the opinion that chances of
success via the routes of official blessing (Spanish or Mexican) might be calculated at something between zero and
none at all.

From a young man whose father owned a rancho not
far from the San José Mission, Bill Beard purchased a worn
saddle and a droopy-eyed gelding with an extremely bad
disposition—and spent most of his time for the next two
weeks attempting to gentle the creature. When he'd succeeded sufficiently so the maverick was actually tractable,
Olivo and Beard (the former on a borrowed but quite
ridable mule) rode back into the hills to the east of the
pueblo, mountains that appeared far more gently config-
ured from a distance than they were in reality. High astride
a bare summit perhaps three thousand feet above the great,
sprawling, nearly lakelike San Francisco Bay, the two men
drew their mounts to a standstill and spent a time gazing off

over flatlands and water and bluegreen mountains to the west and south—the Santa Cruz Range.

"It's a beautiful country, right enough," Beard said—and then whistled.

"Very large," Raymondo Olivo agreed, "mostly in the direction where the sun rises. There is a huge valley beyond these mountains, Guillermo, and beyond the valley is a range of mountains far higher than those we ride upon here. The Californios do not live out in those lands. Only Indios like me, a few of them, but wild, not tame. We could go there—perhaps raise cattle and become rich. We could build a great hacienda and hire priests to clean our stalls . . . But first I must purchase my own freedom. As things are at present, I am like one of the mission cattle."

"Indians?" Bill asked. "Out in the *big* valley—do Ohlones live there also, your people? Costanoans?"

Olivo shook his head.

"I have heard stories, no more," he replied. "Ohlones, Costanoans—they are not one people, linked only by the tongue they speak. Even the language is in many dialects. But these people, *my people*, as you say, they do not live in the great valley. The Indians there are called *Yokuts*, but probably they aren't just one people either."

Sunlight gleamed from the broad blue waters of the bay, and far to the west, sliding over the crests of the mountains, waves of fog splashed silently downward.

"In any case, we've got to have our own land," Beard insisted. "That's the American way. We've got to have *propaty* if we're going to have ourselves a ranch—up against the Santa Cruz Mountains, is what I'd suppose. Inland, that's not so practical. Here we've got oak, madrona, spruce maybe—I don't know. But we'll need timber to build proper houses. And I seem to remember somebody telling me about some red-colored trees roughly the size of whales, or something of that sort. If we're going to get us some land, it's got to have Gawd's own trees growing on it."

"Trees?" Olivo asked. "Americans are strange in the head, I see that now. Obsessed to cut things down. Trees we can have. Indeed, these red-barked trees are much larger than even the greatest whales. But I think we need something else as well. . . ."

"Such as?"

Olivo grinned, leaning forward to rub his mule's ears. "The *beeches*, naturally, the women, *la sexa femenina*. If we are going to build a house, then we must have ladies. For you, it is trees, but for me it is the ladies. In this life, my friend, it's very important to beget children, for in that way a man gains something much like immortality. When a man at last goes to Other Side Camp, his own mother and father and his grandmother and grandfather will all be there. After a time his children will join him."

"Knew I was forgetting some important stuff," Beard scowled. "Truth is, I've been kind of keeping an eye on Señorita Constancia, the little one who works in the *vinedo*. A man can't go to bed with a redwood, after all, even if it's got a fifteen-foot stump, like you say. But what about the wife? Which side's she on?"

"Americans often don't make sense. What are you babbling about, Sancho Beard?"

"When an *Ohlone pilgrim* goes off to Other Side Camp—where's his wife? She already dead, or what?"

"She follows him, of course," Olivo said. "She dies of a broken heart after he's slain attempting to conquer the God of All Redwood Trees."

"I'm glad you could clear up that point. . . ."

"Oh ye of little faith," Olivo nodded. "Yet I tell you something. Constancia—she's nice. But alas, even when the water of the ocean is blue-green and lovely, there is always some terrible fish that rises up to chew off one's leg. You give her your eye, my friend, but she's dangerous. Oh, not the girl herself, you understand? But you've seen her mother, no? Stronger than two men, and has a fine black mustache besides. Whoever weds Señorita Constancia will have to live with *madre politica* also. Then, after a little while, maybe the daughter becomes very like the mother."

"In Vermont we don't let our women gorge, and as a result they don't get fat. So far, so good, eh, companyero? In any case, you sure don't give me much credit, Raymondo

Quixote. In truth, what I had in mind was—well, kidnapping. I've got a feeling Miss Constancia isn't going to object too strenuously when the moment for decision comes around. She likes the cut o' my Yankee jib."

"And after that you keep her skinny—so she don't get to look like Mama? *Amigo*, the friars, they will stretch your neck—after they have cut off your *cabrones*. Indeed, the men of God will find a great tall oak and string you up from one of its limbs. Here in California, we don't court our women in such a manner. Perhaps it's different in Vermont, were you come from?"

"Vermonters don't cotton to kidnapping and rape either," Bill Beard admitted. "I guess nobody does. I'm just babbling, that's all. You sure I have to be responsible for the mother-in-law? That sort of takes the shine off matters, doesn't it?"

Olivo shrugged and then swigged again from the flask.

"Me," he confided, "I watch Señorita Tereza, *sí*, and Señorita Susana also. They're sisters and claim to come from Soledad—both baptized and very good with their Latin, numbers 1002 and 1003. I myself am number 916. Once, my friend, I was called Little Fish Eagle—and I lived in a Saklan village where the two big rivers come together. Ah, that was long ago. I was but a young child then. The priests, they give us food and clothing and shelter, but the brown-robed devils take our names away. Indeed, we become good Catholics, at least on the surface of things, and our souls are said to be saved."

"You think humans actually have souls, do you?"

"*Sí, sí*, very fine souls. But I think Padre Orontes, he may not have one. That's a bad man, Señor Bill. Well, he doesn't concern me—at least not very much. Tereza and Susana, however, they are a different matter. Maybe I watch both of them at the same time."

"That's a thought," Beard nodded, "a genuine thought. The two little fillies get along well, do they?"

"Unfortunately, no. Some ideas, they sound good until a man truly thinks about them."

William Beard chuckled as he savored the image of Raymondo and the two sisters.

"The three of you in the same . . . bed? What are you talking about, man?"

"Have some more wine, *amigo*. When we're up on the mountain this way, we don't have to make sense. But is it not something to think of? Two such ladies at once. . . ."

"And after 1002 and 1003 run you ragged, by God, they can start on each other. Sisterly love, I believe it's called."

"Perverse," Olivo chuckled, "you are very perverse in the mind. *El terquedad grande!*"

"As you said," Beard replied, "when a man's up here on the mountain. . . ."

A week later the American was given the task of driving in a herd of some two hundred longhorns that had been allowed to graze in the *barrancas* to the east of the pueblo—and to this purpose he'd been granted the assistance of half a dozen young mission Indians, two of whom rode while the remaining four went on foot, shod with nothing more than lightweight moccasins. He was dubious, but the four "runners" proved quite adept—and their combined efforts were sufficient to bring the wily longhorned cattle in from the oak and eucalyptus-studded ravines.

Bluegums. Visitors from Australia, permanent aliens. Damned if they don't look like they've been here forever. . . .

It was late afternoon when Beard managed to get the last of the stubborn longhorns into pen areas close by the pueblo, and he proceeded on foot toward the quarters he shared with Raymondo Olivo.

Olivo wasn't at home, but something of a gathering was in progress across the courtyard. Beard ambled on over—and was shocked to find his friend bound to an oak, shirtless. A Leather Jacket officer was in the process of applying a blacksnake to Raymondo's back—while the bound man convulsed with each lash; and with every stroke, yet one more ugly red mark appeared on the flesh.

William Beard took in the scene quickly—Father Orontes standing stiff in his formal black robes, the expression on his face indicative of both sternness and apparent profound satisfaction with what was going on. Several other friars were close about him—and in their midst, peculiarly enough, little 1002, Señorita Tereza. Beard was virtually certain he detected a faint smile on the girl's attractive—even sensuous—brown face.

"*Diez!*" the officer intoned, and with that exclamation turned smartly, saluting in the general direction of the assembled priests, and walked away, pushing carelessly through the throng of Mission Indians who were in obvious forced attendance.

Beard moved forward, glaring momentarily at Orontes and the young Indian girl as well, Tereza standing suspiciously, yes, very odd, close to the good father, right there among the priests—as though enjoying the honor of special status at this rite of flagellation, obviously a time of minor celebration as well as the communal teaching of an object lesson.

Beard wasn't certain as to why, but his intuition told him that the fair señorita had something to do with Olivo's punishment—whether as specific cause or not. If Orontes wanted the girl, was it necessary to brutalize a man whose attentions Tereza had at least tentatively returned? It was a damned show of superior power, pure and simple. Tereza would learn, if she hadn't already, just who was capable of buttering her bread. She, after all, was helpless in the matter—just as Raymondo and all the converted Mission Indians were. If they showed intelligence and a proper disposition, they were given the gift of literacy, complete with Latin and Catholic theology. On the other hand, if their natures didn't lend themselves to the purposes of both indoctrination and education, then indoctrination sufficed—and they became serfs in the most profound sense. Even for such a one as Raymondo, whom the priests had apparently regarded as something of a prodigy, the future remained bleak—the role of a servant, one whose task it was to tend to the needs, both personal and logistical, of his brown-robed Mexican-Spanish mentors.

The entire situation gnawed at something deep down in a Vermonter's being.

"May I assist Raymondo back to his quarters?" Beard inquired of one of the younger priests.

The friar nodded, half sneering, and then turned immediately away, adopting a slow, shuffling walk and keeping his eyes upon the ground.

For his own part, Beard strode to Olivo's side, withdrew a knife, and summarily severed his friend's bindings.

Raymondo was barely conscious, but he nonetheless muttered a feeble "*Gracias.*"

Bill Beard picked up his compadre's coarse linen blouse and helped him into it. Olivo winced, gritted his teeth, attempted to smile.

"What in hell happened. . . . ?"

"Father Orontes, he caught me reading . . . *Don Quixote* . . . I finish early with the clean straw, and so I sat down behind the wheat bins to read. Orontes, he came sneaking in with Tereza. . . . By God, I speak the truth, Señor Bill. Some of these priests, they are little better than village dogs at mating time. They pretend their celibacy, that is all. They make vows to their God, and then they violate those vows. Hypocrisy—public show. I'd have slipped away, but my path was blocked. That damned priest, he has my book, William. I must have it back. The book belongs to—"

Raymondo Olivo had passed out.

His friend lifted him and carried him to the quarters they shared.

Two weeks drifted by since the beating was administered, and Raymondo Olivo was not only fairly well recovered, but even cheerful, though his passion for Tereza, as he was the first to admit, was quelled. Indeed, the lady in question no longer performed her regular duties and was scarcely to be seen at all.

Tereza's sister, Susana, had apparently run away—to escape Orontes's attentions, or so rumor had it. In any case, the girl was gone.

One old woman who had no teeth claimed Susana had been sold to the owner of a hacienda, a transaction not in itself particularly unusual. But if that were the case, the girl's mother apparently wasn't privy to the sale.

During regular hours, Olivo and Beard (still known as Barrington, of course, by the mission priests) went about their assigned tasks as though nothing whatsoever had happened. But the night of the full moon, close to the stroke of midnight, a single candle was lit inside the quarters the two men shared. They moved about quickly, involved with last-minute preparations for an adventure at hand—since, indeed, the slightest omission could well prove disastrous, and they both knew it.

After a few minutes Raymondo snuffed the candle, and the two exited their abode for the last time. Keeping well to the shadows, they made their way to the rectory, to the quarters of none other than Father Orontes himself.

"You realize," Beard whispered, "we're dead men if we're caught. We could still just take some horses and get the hell out of here. I don't know who's the greater fool—you, for taking such a chance to get your wretched book back, or me for going along with your wild idea. . . ."

"You make too much noise, Sancho," Olivo replied. "If it were not only your book, but also your back that had borne the whip, would you do less? *La venganza*, it's necessary to a man's honor. I tell you, life's worth nothing without *la venganza*."

William Beard studied the shadows for some hint of movement—of danger from a Leather Jacket guard.

"To die for a book that ain't even written in English?" Beard replied. "A heathen Spanish book? Now if it were *Rasselas* or *The Canterbury Tales*, then I could almost go along with you. Tell you what, Ray. If we live through this business, I'll buy you a dozen first-rate books. English books, by Gawd, written in a genuine, civilized language."

"I have heard of these *Canterbury Tales*, my friend.

Also, if I may point out the obvious, Señor Beard, you are indeed and without question going along with me."

"Right, right. Sorta slipped my mind there, Raymond. Look who's up ahead."

One Leather Jacket was sprawled in sleep against a wooden column in the main hallway. As partners in crime, Olivo and Beard quickly overpowered the hapless Mexican soldier, first rendering him unconscious and then binding and gagging him and relieving him both of his weapon and of the ring of keys he carried.

With the guard out of their way, Olivo and Beard moved directly to the door of Orontes' private quarters. The two men required but a moment to deduce the correct key, and with it they entered.

They were not, however, quite prepared for what they now saw—a spectacle illumined by perhaps a dozen candles placed in a double row the width of an inlaid oaken table, at the center of which a copy of the *Holy Bible* lay open, a velvet marker diagonally across its pages. On the wall, to one side of the table, hung the head priest's habit.

Orontes, presently clad only in white linen and clearly not wearing a hair shirt of any sort, sat on the edge of a large, sumptuously canopied bed. The good father's eyes were closed, and his mouth was partially open—as though the man were enthralled in a profound trance. With one hand he clasped a bedpost, while with the other he clung to the long, lustrous black hair of a naked woman—one whom both Olivo and Beard immediately and correctly presumed to be the unfortunate concubine, Tereza.

4

Going Where God's
Trees Grow

Orontes, as yet unaware of his visitors, muttered between gasps of pleasure, "This act will . . . purify . . . your pagan soul, my child. . . ."

The young woman, with perhaps more skill than enthusiasm, was using not only her hands but also her mouth to manipulate the priest's *varilla*.

"Ah, Tereza!" Raymondo hissed, "how can you play the *puta* with so foul a beast? Perhaps I should kill the holy man and his plaything as well? I owe this priest something, sweet Jesus have mercy upon me. I thirst for *sangre*. . . ."

Bill Beard strode immediately forward and pressed the barrel of his horse pistol against Father Orontes' temple. The Indian girl pulled away in silent fright, scrambling on hands and knees, and, absurd though the act might have been, attempting, with a coverlet from the priest's bed, to hide her nakedness. The extent of her movements were limited, however, for indeed she was chained to a bedpost by means of a silver gyve about her slim left ankle.

Orontes drew in his breath, coughed—indeed as though he'd been dreaming some Great Satanic Dog had him by the leg. In less than an instant, however, he lost all interest in being nibbled at, and his manhood wilted—as

45

though it had been some worm-eaten toadstool, necrotic after heavy rains.

Señorita Tereza cowered on the floor but did not speak. After his initial outburst, Raymondo chose to ignore her completely.

"Señor Orontes," Olivo said as he held out a candle-stick at arm's length, half threatening to thrust the flame into the priest's face, "I have come to borrow back that book of mine. Surely you are through with it by now. . . . As for this woman—Tereza, is it? I may have cared for her once, but now she is spoiled, and I no longer have any interest in her."

"What are you . . . men doing . . . here in my . . . quarters?" Orontes sputtered. "In the name of the Holy of Holies, I'll have you both drawn and quartered and hung into the bargain."

"No, no, by the Mother of God," Olivo replied. "I don't think so. I know a priest of the Jesus Church would never lie, not even to a poor Ohlone Indian like me, and yet I think, Padre Orontes, you cannot foresee the future any better than another man. We all walk upon two feet, is it not so? Please, therefore, to give me the book—for other-wise, my friend Barrington here, he will cut off your *bolas* and then he will slit your miserable throat."

Orontes was on the verge of objecting, but then he took careful note of the weapon in the American's hand— and so he reconsidered the matter. He rose stiffly, and, with Beard close behind him, walked to a considerable book-shelf, reached up, and took down a copy of *Don Quixote*.

"Inferior edition," he muttered. "Pirated no doubt."

"*Amable, amable*," Olivo nodded, "*gracias*. I want only what is rightfully mine. One further thing. Please to give me the key to Tereza's manacle. Whatever else she may be, she is not a wild coyote to be kept on the end of a chain."

The priest shrugged, gestured to where a small skele-ton key dangled from a loop of gold braid.

"Now," Orontes began, attempting as well as his circumstances might allow to summon a degree of dignity, "if you men will be so kind as to be on your way. . . ."

"Just what we had in mind," Beard chuckled. "Only thing is—I guess you have to come with us, Padre. A moonlight ride will do you good. . . ."

"Señor Barrington, I beg of you. Please recall the kindnesses I have done in your behalf."

"Nothing shall be forgotten," Beard assured him.

"Ten, fifteen miles," Olivo added. "Then we leave you—with no clothes, barefoot. Or perhaps we will just stick a knife into your big belly. Who can say?"

He looked down at Tereza, who in turn smiled vacuously.

"Raymondo . . . ?" she entreated.

"Little one, you're like some dog that's caught eating the droppings of a pig," Olivo said, shrugging and gesturing with his copy of *Don Quixote*. "It has been the fate of our people, Tereza, yours and mine. We must learn to stand on our own feet, all of us, so that when the Great Dreamer chooses to change things once again, he will remember who we are. I will free you, but I will not take you with me to a place of freedom. No, I think it's up to you whether you allow yourself to be bound in this way again."

With a fine string of some seventeen horses in tow and plentiful moonlight to facilitate the journey, William Beard (late of the *Pride*) and Raymondo Olivo (late of the Mission Santa Clara de Guadalupe) traveled southward, skirting several tidewater swamps at the bay's terminus.

At length they drew to a halt. Both Orontes and Tereza (Baptism Number 1002) were left on foot, the priest being allowed, despite earlier threats, to retain his habit and his bootkins as well. Tereza, now clad in the usual garb allowed to Mission Indian girls, was provided with a half-sword previously taken from the Leather Jacket soldier who'd been left bound and gagged at the mission.

"*Buenas noches, hasta la vista,*" Olivo called out. "Ah Tereza! Once I loved you, yes, you and your sister as well, but no more. Kill the fat priest if he does not please you. Doubtless his god will carry him off to heaven in any case, though possibly Señor . . . Barrington and I ought to provide some assistance by way of tying him to a tree and driving nails through the palms of his hands. . . ."

"Surely you would never perform so barbaric a *movimiento*," Orontes said, his voice now utterly subdued. "Such a thing would be contrary to everything you learned at the mission. . . ."

"*Sí*, yes, I learned many things from you. I learned to be tied to a tree and whipped. Perhaps a few lashes across your backside. . . ."

"Or we could just turn them loose," Beard suggested. "The way I see it, they pretty much deserve each other."

Neither Orontes nor the firm-breasted Tereza saw fit to make any response whatsoever—the priest doubtlessly pleased at being still alive, and not wishing to risk further antagonizing his former captors. But as for the Indian girl, who could say?

Olivo and Beard moved their small herd of horses onward, even past the point where it was clear the animals wished to rest. The creatures were definitely becoming somewhat balky and had begun to demonstrate a tendency toward straying. Finally the cohorts reached a point where the occasionally traveled wagon trail they followed began its ascent into the mountains of Santa Cruz, and here they allowed their purloined animals to drink and graze for a short time.

When a few horses demonstrated a distinct inclination toward bedding down for what remained of the night, the conspirators urged the remuda into motion once more— southward, upslope now, and into a region of numerous arroyos and thick oak woods, these blending by degrees into stands of fir, pine, and redwood as the herd of stolen horses traversed onward. When at last stars began to vanish and the sky changed to a soft silver color, with whiteness running to pale violet along the eastward horizon, the remuda was high in the mountains. Where a small stream cascaded from dense forest on the slope above, Beard called a halt for the purpose of resting the animals.

"Faithful guide," he called to Olivo, "is it a good idea to continue along this roadway? Aren't we likely within an hour or so to meet someone coming the other direction? Since we've only recently gained possession of these fine *caballos*, perhaps we should turn up a side canyon and find a meadow where the allies of Father Orontes will not discover us—for surely that pig of a priest will send out a band of Leather Jackets to murder us and to seize our horses. What sayest thou, my leader?"

"Perhaps Tereza has had the good sense to stick him in the throat. No matter, no matter. I have a better idea," Olivo said after a moment's consideration. "We'll search for an Indian village. I have heard of a chief known as Pelican Doctor—one who's kept his people away from the Spanish priests, though he himself was captured by them when he was but a young man. When he had learned of the ways of the Spanish and knew how to use their weapons, he returned to his own village—or so the story runs. It's said that he and his people have guns, and so neither the Leather Jackets nor the Californio ranchers dare to bother them. If Pelican Doctor doesn't kill us immediately and declare a celebration and roast us for dinner, Guillermo my partner, then I think he may protect us from our enemies. With a few of these horses, we'll pay him for protection."

"Pelican Doctor, eh? And what if this relative of yours decides to murder us and simply take our horses?"

"He's no relative of mine, Bill—I explained all that to you before. You must learn to listen. You make a good point, nonetheless."

"Well?"

"Then we'll be dead, of course. When a man is dead, he does not have to worry about anything."

"Damned comforting, Raymond," Beard replied. "It's good to know I'm always able to rely on you for common-sense philosophy. Onward, then, Don Quick-shoat. I'll Sancho at your side for a bit longer. I mean, hell, get right down to it, what are my alternatives?"

"It's my fate," Olivo laughed, "to lead crazy Americans to where the great trees grow. I'm like St. Christopher. The weight of my burden is terrible."

By mid-morning they reached a pass through the mountains. Perhaps fifteen miles to the south a heavy sheet of low cloud abutted the land, obscuring both the seaward plain and the ocean itself. The general lay of the terrain, however, was hardly a mystery to Bill Beard—for, as would have been the case with any good Yankee sailor in similar circumstances, he'd made careful note of a chart that adorned the whitewashed adobe wall of the mission's chapel anteway.

Thus far in their journey, they'd met no one coming from the opposite direction. Wishing no human contact, they turned their horses northwest and followed the general rim of the Santa Cruz Mountains, skirting an occasional peak but otherwise staying to the back of the range for a dozen miles or more and only then proceeding downslope along a canyon whose drainage seemed destined to reach the Pacific Ocean itself. Below them grew dense stands of redwood trees, tall and graceful even if not of the gigantic proportions Raymondo had once described.

"Whatever sort of future awaits us," Beard laughed as they drew up on the reins of their mounts, "I guess it lies downslope. Look, Raymondo. The ocean out there—big and silver-gray and bursting with light. Takes a while for the fogs to burn off in this region, as I gather, but I should say it's worth the wait."

"You're thinking of being back on some ship, perhaps? Me, I wish merely to stay ashore. Yes. Down below us somewhere must be Pelican Doctor's village—except, of course, that Ohlones move their villages from time to time. Some village sites are more or less permanent, while others are temporary—for hunting or for fishing. In any case, I've never come here before. My friend, possibly I should have been more temperate in my judgment of Señorita Tereza. After all, she did only what she was obliged to do—however angry I may have become to see her doing it. But now I'm lonely and very tired and I wish she were with me. Perhaps she'd do for me what she did for the corrupt priest. . . ."

"Don't think so," Beard replied. "That big-gutted padre wouldn't have moved in on her, not unless she encouraged him to some extent. That's what my Yankee intuition tells me, at least. Maybe I'm wrong. . . ."

"How reliable a faculty is this *Yankee intuition*? No matter. We must ride down into the canyons now. Pelican Doctor or no Pelican Doctor, our horses require not only forage, but also water. The *barranca* ahead of us—I think it will afford us passage and not demand broken legs of our horses, for that would be a toll no traveler would wish to pay."

"You get the feeling," Beard suggested as they thumped their heels to the ponies' sides, "that maybe we didn't think our escape plan through as well as we might have? Will we be able to sell the animals in Branciforte?"

"A *posibilidad*, yes. Bill, I am very tired. Indeed, I would give almost anything to be back in our comfortable little hovel. I suppose there's some reason why we cannot make our camp right here?"

"Not yet, Raymondo, not yet. Once we've reached the bottom of this canyon, we'll be out of harm's way. . . ."

Positioning their mounts around behind the band of horses, they moved forward, propelling their balky charges once more into action. The shallow ravine, without running water and offering nothing beyond an occasional swampy area, provided exactly the passageway they sought. Within half an hour, herd intact, they reached a stream and entered in under a high green canopy of redwood foliage. The trees here were indeed large—nearly as great as those in Raymondo's imagination—and stunningly tall. Late afternoon sunlight seemed to cascade from the high boughs as though some sort of dazzling yellow snowstorm were in silent progress.

A good-sized creek coiled among boulders, the waters lined by pale-barked alders standing to either side of the creek. Between groves of giant redwoods were areas of

meadow, clearings lush with grass, occasional bunchings of
dark green fern, and thick tangles of willow and aromatic
laurel.

From his saddlebags, Olivo withdrew a slab of corned
beef (courtesy of the good friars of San Jose), a loaf of hard
bread, and a full wineskin besides. Beard managed to get a
fire going, and soon the men were sprawled out, one to
either side of the small blaze. They passed the wineskin
back and forth, chewed on beef and bread, and watched as
the western sky first went dull crimson and then silver and
then black—a blackness punctuated between the spires of
great trees, with an occasional burst of stars. A warm
current of air flowed down from the mountains, and a
horned owl called mournfully, in apparent hope of companionship.

"By Gawd," Bill mused, "this is what I was missing all
those months—no, years—on the high seas. The feel of
good, solid earth beneath my bones! I tell you, Ray, it's only
when a man's had the earth itself taken away from him for
a spell that he truly comes to appreciate 'er. One thing's for
certain. If your friend Pelican Doctor's anywhere along
this canyon, our smoke's going to go right down to him—as
certain as though it were government mail. The truth is,
though—I don't really figure there are any other human
beings within thirty miles of us. Yes sir. The trees are
damned near as big as you said they were going to be, and
we've got 'em all to ourselves. Once we've found a hardware store where we can buy us a couple of good Vermont
axes, we can start chopping. Hell, we'll have this place
cleared out in no time. . . ."

"*Desde luego*, naturally. Sometimes I worry about you,
Sancho Bill. Or are you Don Quixote himself, while I am
but the faithful Sancho? I suppose we'll be able to tell when
we come to the place of the windmills."

Olivo rose, stretched his arms above his head, and
walked over to where the saddlebags hung. He retrieved
his precious copy of *Don Quixote*, returned to the fireside,
sat down once more, and attempted to read a few pages.

Occasionally he glanced at his American friend, grinned, and shook his head.

"Lord," Bill Beard groaned, "here I am in an Indian-infested wilderness, and my only human companion's gone utterly mad. So tell me about these . . . Ohlones. The village you came from—it was related or not? I take it you'll at least be able to understand this Pelican Doctor, in case we meet up with the gentleman?"

Feigning exasperation, Raymondo put his book aside. He picked up a pebble and used forefinger and thumb to flick the bit of stone off toward the stream.

"Of course, *ciertamente*," he laughed. "It is said Pelican Doctor speaks Spanish, though probably I will be able to communicate in Ohlone dialect also."

Bill nodded, stared into the fire.

"Are the Ohlones . . . God-fearing people? I mean, how do they figure they got here?"

"I was young when the padres took me to the mission," Olivo replied, "and yet I remember quite a few things. For a long time I promised myself I would learn whatever the Spanish God-men had to teach me, and then I would return to Saklan. Here's one story. Then I'm going to turn over and go to sleep."

"Fair enough. An Injun tale, right?"

Olivo took another swig from the wineskin and passed the leather container back to Beard.

"In the beginning—just as in *Genesis*—the entire world was covered with water. Next a single mountain rose from the flood—for my people, that was *Monte Diabolo*, which was named by the Spaniards because they thought my people believed the peak to be inhabited by spirits. Perhaps for the Indios in this area where we are now, some other high place stood above the ocean of long ago. I have heard of something like that about Pico Blanco, off to the south, beyond Río Sur, though I've never been there. Now I'll tell the story. You see, Coyote and Eagle and Hummingbird sat together on Monte Diabolo, and after the water went away, Eagle directed that the Ohlones be created. Then Uncle Coyote married the first woman.

Sometimes he went after other women as well. Often he succeeded, and once in a while he was defeated. Yet that never matters to Coyote, for he's the one who brought culture—he set up all the villages and the other tribes as well, and he showed the people how to secure food. He showed us how to build houses and how to make tools and weapons—and even how to pry abalones from the rocks. Señor Beard, leave a little wine for me, *por favor.*"

Bill Beard handed Raymondo the flask. Again he drank, returned the now relatively flaccid wineskin, and put his head into his hands, as though in contemplation.

Beard also drank, waited patiently for a long minute or two before speaking.

"What the hell you being so meditative about, anyhow? Still mooning over that little Number 1002? Once a gal goes bad, Raymondo, there's no help for it. Ain't that right? Little Tereza wanted Saint Tubaguts, and now she's got him."

Olivo's only answer was a sort of snuffling snore.

"Sound asleep." Beard chuckled. "Some fellas just don't have any endurance—just can't hold their ale. Surely I'm not going to have to tuck you in, Raymondo, old companyero. . . ."

But then Olivo turned over onto his side, drew his blanket about his shoulders and wheezed contentedly.

Beard listened to rhythmically repeated, lonely cries of the horned owl and, catching the faint reply of another bird of the same variety much farther back up into the canyon, he smiled into the darkness.

This was, indeed, a beautiful country—this land of California—even if it did lie three thousand miles distant from Vermont. Three thousand, hell—make it fifteen thousand, since that was the way he'd come: clear down to the Straits of Magellan (where penguins stood about on the shore and gazed out haughtily) and then back north along the entire extent of South America (the huge Andes Mountains lifting up into the clouds) and along half of North America as well.

What were the chances of eventual Yankee settlement

in California? The possibility of such a thing, doubtless, was very slim, though if the Mexicans succeeded in their present war with Spain, was it not merely a matter of time until this neglected northern extension of Mexico in turn sought to throw off the bonds that held it in uneasy alliance to a mother country far to the south? To the north were the British of Hudson's Bay Company. Even the Russkies, or so he'd been told, had gained a minor toehold not too far beyond Yerba Buena.

With standing timber of the sort that grew in the Sierra Santa Cruz, and with even greater forests reputed in the mountainous regions both north of Yerba Buena and south along the Ventana coast, a significant timber industry might be founded, one that could rival the operations in the Maine woods. But where was such sawn timber to be sold? To the settlements of the western coast of South America, perhaps, or in the Sandwich Islands? As it was, the extremely sparse population of Alta California hardly justified anything beyond the cutting of individual trees, as necessity dictated.

After taking yet one more swig from the wineskin and wondering how to go about procuring further supplies of the elixir of the grape, after wondering why it was that he, unlike his friend Raymondo Quixote Olivo, was not tired—William Beard closed his eyes as though to rest them momentarily, and then he too rolled over, drew his robe about his shoulders, and slept profoundly.

Dawn in the redwood canyon came in a suffused burst of pale crimson above black-shadowed forms of the trees—light and intertwined odors of running water and mist and ferns and late-blooming buckeye and mock orange. Half a dozen tule elk glided away, startled at the smell of human creatures, and vanished into dense forest cover. Bluejays cried out and danced the air from one redwood to another.

Trills of screech owls, unusual during morning hours. . . .

If it wasn't that, then something else awakened the Yankee—perhaps a sense of human presence. Groggily

Beard reached for his pistol, was unable to determine where he'd placed the weapon, and then sat up.

The sound of hooves striking on spongy ground—and then he saw them, realized what was happening. The string of horses he and Raymondo had liberated were in the process of fleeing from their benefactors. The creatures were in full flight, pouring across a narrow meadow and swerving only slightly as they went around the spot where the partners were camped. Within moments the seventeen ponies vanished amongst thick growth downstream.

Both Olivo and Beard were on their feet now, only to be confronted by a broad-shouldered, heavily muscled individual whose age, Beard estimated, must have been in the vicinity of half a century. The Indian wore a small basket hat adorned with numerous feathers—while from under the hat's brim a profusion of long, silver-tinged hair poured forth. The man's oval-shaped brown face was wrinkled, but dark eyes, flickering from Olivo to Beard, were intense with life. Indeed, the face seemed all but Oriental, while his deep-set, brooding, heavy-lidded eyes beneath thick eyebrows gave the Indian leader almost the appearance of a Celestial wise man. The remainder of his costume consisted of a leather breechclout and moccasins whose uppers reached to the calf and were cross-laced. Both arms were tattooed with series of wavy, parallel dots. He held a pistol—not threateningly but as if a matter of formality. His smile seemed neither practiced nor particularly friendly.

"You are surrounded, *para encierro*," the imposing Indian said in Spanish. "For this reason, I do not believe it would be wise for you men to attempt to escape. We've already taken your weapons—we did this while you slept. After all, we don't wish you to shoot anybody. I am Pelican Doctor. Come now. My men and I will take you to our village, to *la aldea Hotochruk*. Your horses will be there when we arrive—don't worry about them. My people won't eat horseflesh. I give you my word. But you must tell me where you were going with so many *caballos*. Maybe you steal them from Pueblo Branciforte?"

Olivo was about to speak, but Pelican Doctor turned

away abruptly—making clear that his question had been uttered for reasons purely rhetorical.

A dozen Ohlone warriors, most of them armed with short bows or with spears, now pressed in about the partners. The Indians eased into a slow run, and thus the two erstwhile liberators of horses had little choice but to move along in unison with their captors.

"Raymondo," Beard managed, "I do believe we've been had. Ohlones . . . aren't known for cannabalism . . . are they? A fine bunch of relatives you've got. . . ."

"Keep running, Guillermo. Don't let them think you're growing tired."

"Usually you've *got a better idea*. Well . . . ?"

"I will try . . . to think . . . of one," Raymondo Olivo replied.

5

Daughters to Pelican Doctor

For reasons best known to himself, Pelican Doctor decided not to have the American and his tame Indian partner dispatched. Instead, the chief provided the captive pair with sleeping pallets inside his own dwelling. Thus it was that Raymondo Olivo and William Beard came to be unwilling guests of the chief of the Hotochruk Ohlones—and, by means of proximity, guests also of the twin daughters, Seagull and Calling Owl.

The girls' mother had died seven years earlier, possibly of the pox (as Beard judged details of the chief's story), and so the two young women stayed on with their father, growing to adulthood. They were now some eighteen years of age, slim, taller than Olivo himself, fine-featured, remarkably agile, and, by anybody's standards, damned attractive. For two eligible and decidedly randy bachelors to find themselves in close contact with a pair of sensuous lookalikes was trying, to say the least, especially since the continued goodwill of Pelican Doctor was literally a matter of life and death—and since the young ladies in question began to show definite signs of being favorably inclined toward such advances as Raymondo and Guillermo might eventually wish to make.

Seagull was the more serious of the two young women and somewhat less talkative—though in fact there was little to choose between the ladies. For whatever reasons, however, Seagull seemed to be interested in Beard, while Calling Owl preferred Raymondo. All for the better, as Beard supposed—since in this way, Pelican Doctor would be required to put both men to death, and not just one or the other, should it come to that. But the ladies, as matters turned out, were clearly the aggressors in the ritual of courtship that was to follow.

Raymondo believed that this sensuous fruit, however available, should remain unplucked, inasmuch as it was doubtlessly interdicted. Often he reminded Beard of the fate of Adam and Eve in the book of *Genesis*, and even though the American consistently pointed out the inappropriateness of the analogy, Raymondo would merely grimace and mumble, "Doesn't matter. Yankees never understand anything important. . . ."

Respect for Pelican Doctor, however, and for his authority as well, seemed to preclude following the amorous path indicated, even though Seagull and Calling Owl persisted in subtle but definite come-hither gestures such as those made, Raymondo explained, by Indian women who wished to be courted for marriage. In some relatively essential ways, Beard concluded, things were not altogether different in California—though the signals the women sent were far more obvious than would have been the case in Vermont.

Was it possible, after all, that Pelican Doctor had decided to convert his two captives into a pair of son-in-laws?

A few other matters as well differed from what the man from Vermont was used to—though Olivo made assurances that very much the same practices were in force in the village from which he himself had come.

Beard nodded. He'd seen enough of the world so that he felt no need to be surprised. The men of Hotochruk went naked when the weather permitted, while the women wore two short skirts, one before and one behind. These garments were made of bark fiber, woven tules, or deer-skin. Quite often the women went about bare-breasted, though not always, and many sported facial tattoos—either lines or rows of dots.

Oddly enough, neither Seagull nor Calling Owl had been tattooed—and Beard surmised that Pelican Doctor, having spent time among the friars of Santa Cruz, might possibly have concluded that comeliness among women wasn't essentially dependent upon the practice of self-mutilation—though from his own tattoos, it was clear that the chief hardly despised the practice.

The entire situation was vexing.

In the first place, Pelican Doctor had remarked (casu-ally enough) that general practice in war precluded the taking of prisoners. In the case of exceptions to the rule, captives such as Olivo and Beard were traditionally dis-patched as soon as possible. Had the pair been mere Spaniards or Mexicans, the old chief grinned, they would have been bound to a bay tree so that the children might practice their stone-throwing.

But then the chief explained that some in the village wished him to take another wife—so that he might beget a son who'd eventually become the new chief. Pelican Doc-tor, however, was not inclined to take a woman. One mate, the old villain laughed, had been quite sufficient. Several widows in his village were willing to lie down with him when he was afflicted by the madness of desire. He saw no need to complicate his life further. In any case, if he remarried and eventually sired another half-dozen chil-dren, these might well all turn out to be girls—and so his peace of mind would have been destroyed for nought. Soon his twin daughters would take husbands and would give him grandchildren. Perhaps a grandson could be the next chief. And yet there were several young men among the warriors who were natural leaders and would be able to guide the people, when the appropriate time came.

Did these casual remarks suggest that Pelican Doctor meant for the chieftainship to be passed along to one of his eventual son-in-laws? Had the chief, in fact, welcomed the strangers into his home so that one or the other might become that son-in-law? If true, then Raymondo was the obvious candidate. . . . Or was the chief simply testing the men—willing to put them summarily to death should they abuse the hospitality he'd shown—by virtue (or lack thereof) of attempting to have their way with his lovely, bare-breasted twin daughters, Seagull and Calling Owl?

Conjecture, in fact, ran through the entire village, for no one in Hotochruk seemed quite certain what their chief's strange behavior indicated.

Pelican Doctor hadn't returned the pair's weapons, although he'd otherwise allowed Olivo and Beard the run of the village and the forest that surrounded it. Adolescent boys were entrusted with the responsibility of watching over the small herd of horses, but Beard and Olivo's riding ponies had been returned, thus granting significant freedom of movement—apparently including escape, should the prisoners desire it.

Rather than leave Hotochruk, however, Raymondo and Guillermo stayed on with Pelican Doctor—at the same time continuing to act politely and reservedly toward the twins. The partners had reason to suppose, after all, that Californio authorities might wish to hang them, should they show their faces in the vicinity of any of the missions or pueblos. Father Orontes was likely to order brutal whippings and then to forgive sins and then to demand that necks be stretched.

The big trees continued to exercise their power over the practical New England imagination of William Beard. As the Vermonter considered matters, so astonishing a resource could hardly continue to go unused. Indeed, the entire future of this land of California might well depend as much upon the dark and prolix forests as upon the astonishingly rich soil. Was it not man's moral duty to tame the wilderness and to spread civilization across the land? To bring the light to all areas of darkness?

In order to do so, one would be obliged to cut down a few trees and to saw them into lumber.

With these and similar considerations in mind, Beard proceeded to make careful survey of the redwood forest surrounding the Ohlone village. First he determined the essential properties of the wood—from downfall logs which, self-evidently lying in place for an indeterminate number of years, remained unrotted, apparently owing to some naturally occurring preservative within the wood itself. The material was light, relatively strong, apparently all but invulnerable to rot, resistant even to fire, but with a tendency toward brittleness. Redwood would clearly not do for ships' masts; but for carpentry, Beard concluded, it should prove excellent.

The big trees apparently grew best in canyons—for the true giants were generally restricted to such zones. Beyond that, the trees seemed to flourish only in those areas where mists most commonly drifted in off the ocean, morning and evening fogs which the trees were somehow able to milk—upper boughs collecting moisture which then, upon gathering, dripped down to the floor of the forest, keeping the underlying carpet of needles damp except during occasional brilliant intervals of midday sunlight.

Indeed, to walk among the redwoods, many of them surely in excess of two hundred feet tall, and a few probably three hundred or even more, was almost to have passed into a realm of dream, or myth, of timelessness. The redwood forests were, Beard fancied, strewn segments of some long-lost Garden of Eden. Nor was the effect produced merely by the mighty trees themselves, their tops seemingly lost in a blur of sunlight. Pink and white azaleas bloomed in the understory, with faint, honeyed odor drifting on cool air. Ferns were everywhere, along with startlingly profuse rhododendrons, sorrels, trilliums, wild tulips, skunk cabbage, bush and ground lupines, buckeye, wild lilac, aromatic bay trees, and nutmegs. In addition there were gnarled canyon liveoaks, black oaks, and pines, while up on the sharp ridges between drainages were thick groves of firs whose height and girth, in scattered instances, rivaled the redwoods themselves.

To proceed inland was to pass out of groves of redwoods and to emerge at length on the high, grassy backs of these Santa Cruz Mountains. From such a point one might gaze inland across yet further forests of pine and oak and Australian blue gum, the latter (or so the story went) an accidental gift of British sailors stopping along the coast for tanbark oak and leaving behind, a century past, a few scattered handfuls of eucalyptus seeds—the dense, flourishing groves sloping down to the southern end of Bahía del San Francisco, across whose waters, faintly visible, were the San José mission and pueblo, presided over by the corrupt Fray Orontes—unless, of course, Fair Tereza had been inspired to stick her knife into the lecher's bloated belly.

Olivo and Beard traversed the ridges both north and south, discovering some truly memorable groves of big trees—as well as significant stands of pine and fir, oak and madroña. Bill Beard began to think seriously of the possibility of setting up some kind of mill—a shingle mill, perhaps, or a makeshift arrangement to hew out timbers that might be sold in Santa Cruz or Monterey—or even, eventually, to be shipped elsewhere to market.

The one issue that most troubled his inherently practical Yankee soul, however, was that of right and wrong. Indeed, the scheme of felling such huge and doubtlessly ancient trees seemed all but immoral. But such a response was, he realized, simply emotional—and one should never allow one's emotions to overcome one's business common sense. Hadn't the Lord God put all of creation in place for the proper uses of His human creatures? These huge trees would indeed test a man's mettle—would prove him sufficient, were he able to convert them to the needs of commerce.

Even as such thoughts passed through his mind, however, he was aware that the line of argumentation—of utility over aesthetics—had never before in his life persuaded him of anything. It was not practicality, needless to say, that had sent him out to adventure upon the high seas. And as to the presumed purposes of the Lord God—in fact, Beard had long since concluded that all proper, church-going folk (such as he'd been raised among in New England) were a tad touched in the head, folk who channeled their private insanities into the realm of what they chose to believe was religion. Get right down to it, or so he believed, that kind of faith was little more than a childish desire to have things governed by heavenly parents—yes, and a crazed notion that death and hence extinction might somehow, miraculously, be avoided by means of professing to believe that one particular man of questionable legitimacy had been conceived by a God with an eye toward mortal women, that this man once walked upon water, and that he'd subsequently risen from the dead, thus having *saved* all *true believers*.

Perhaps one would do better to consult the Tio Coyote Raymondo professed to believe in. If to anyone, then these trees surely belonged to the whimsical God-beast— since Coyote was the one who'd presumably created the redwoods—and had gotten carried away and made them considerably larger than the Great Dreamer intended.

Intriguing idea. . . . Handyman to the Divine, with a will of his own, a sense of humor, a sense of whimsy. . . . May the Good Lord forgive this wretched sinner for the blasphemous maunderings of a crazed mind.

Religion aside, Beard now wondered whether he or anyone else had the moral right to fell the huge trees that grew in these mist-filled California canyons.

Leave the hugest of 'em, he mused, and cut their lesser relatives. Truth is, it'd take a team of giants to cut the big fellows in any case. The proper size for logs is no more than a team of Clydesdales can skid along. . . .

The village of Hotochruk itself was situated in a meadow where two great redwoods grew amidst a scattering of their lesser sisters—perhaps a mile or so downstream from a waterfall that cascaded from a slot in the rocks where stone itself took on the appearance of some powerful chief, one of the "ancient ones," as Pelican Doctor remarked.

Hotochruk was arranged in a series of concentric circles, the houses constructed of poles covered with brush, tule matting, and strips of redwood bark—the latter evidently skinned away from fallen trees. Pelican Doctor's lodge was somewhat different, much taller than the others and conical in form, with slender poles and withes holding the thatch together from the outside, against an interior framework. Not far from the chief's dwelling stood the medicine lodge, a domelike affair sheathed almost entirely by segments of redwood bark. Finally, close to the stream was a sweat lodge that received frequent use.

A mile below the village, the stream along whose banks Hotochruk had been built found its way to yet another creek of the same size, and together the melded waters wandered an additional mile or two to the extremities of the last waning ridge of the mountains and onward to the dunes and cliff faces abutting the gray-green Pacific Ocean.

The village was hidden—away from an infrequently used horse trail that led from Santa Cruz Mission northward to a way station at Half Moon Bay and thence to Mission Dolores, Yerba Buena, and Bahía del San Francisco. Originally, Pelican Doctor informed his house guests, Hotochruk had been much closer to Santa Cruz, but as a result of the village having twice been raided by Mexican Leather Jacket soldiers, the previous chief had found it expedient and wise to remove to this present location.

Pelican Doctor himself, as a boy, had been captured by Spanish-Mexicans in one of those raids, and for some four years he was held as a virtual prisoner. Only because he'd learned that a similar fate had befallen Raymondo Olivo, or so the chief said, had he ultimately chosen to spare the lives of the two captives—horse thieves, as he supposed. In any case, Pelican Doctor eventually escaped from the mission and returned, searching back into each *barranca* where the great trees grew until he managed to discover the whereabouts of the Hotochrukma, his people—who, in turn,

viewed his appearance as nothing less than a miracle. For a
time, no doubt, some of the Ohlones actually supposed
their future chief to have come back from Other Side
Camp—from death itself, doubtless with the direct assistance of Trickster Coyote.

Not only had the boy returned, but he'd brought with
him a pistol and a goodly quantity of ammunition. The
Mexican soldier whose weapon the pistol had originally
been, Pelican Doctor explained, had no more use for
it—inasmuch as the man was dead. Pelican Doctor's knife
somehow lodged itself in the Leather Jacket's throat, and,
the soldier having given up the ghost, the boy proceeded to
scalp the man—a *full scalp*, face and all, in effect skinning
the Leather Jacket's head.

As years went by and the old chief died and passed on
into the Spirit World—with Pelican Doctor becoming the
new leader—other weapons came into the possession of the
Hotochrukma: a brace of fusees, three Mexican military
flintlock rifles, and a multishot British pepperbox pistol.
Powder and lead as well were acquired, and great care was
taken to see to it that this magic substance remained dry
and protected.

Mexican law, of course, forbade Indios to possess
firearms, on pain of public flogging or possibly execution by
firing squad. But while it was well-known by those at
Branciforte that Pelican Doctor and his people had firearms, the two attempts to retrieve the guns from these
recalcitrant wild people resulted in a total of thirteen
Leather Jackets dead, their mutilated bodies left close
beside the horse trail from Santa Cruz to Yerba Buena.

The most recent of the encounters had occurred no
more than a month prior to the "arrest" of Beard and Olivo
by the Hotochrukma.

Given the circumstances, Beard could well imagine
that the prospect of a campaign against these wild people
would hardly have been popular among either the troops or
their commanding officers. Nor were the good priests
particularly eager to save Hotochrukman souls. One might
as well attempt to convert *Ursa horribilis*, the grizzly bear.

The Santa Cruz Mountains remained under the control of Pelican Doctor and his Ohlone warriors—and, of course, the great golden grizzlies, the mountain lions who screamed at night, the yowling wolves and coyotes, the mighty-winged condors, the turkey vultures and redtailed hawks and bald and golden eagles, and along the beaches, huge male sea lions, groaning and roaring, as the urge took them.

The impact of civilization upon this beautiful land where gigantic redwoods huddled in astonishing groves back up in the canyons was, succinctly put, somewhere between little and none.

Bill Beard, after all, claimed to be a proper (if somewhat eccentric) Vermonter—one who'd grown up close by the logging woods, one who'd worked with axe and saw and peavey in the days before he'd given in to the lure of the sea.

In New England, agriculture demanded a preliminary clearing of the forest as well as the picking up of endless bushels of stones, these tucked into walls that went everywhere. But such was hardly the case in California. Indeed, the land was amazingly fertile, and considerable portions were both flat and grassy. Up on the mountainsides, however, impressive forests grew. On the lowlands, if stories were to be believed, snow never fell—and even frost was highly unusual. In the mountains, though, snow did fall at higher elevations, feeding streams that ran throughout long and rainless summers.

A strange place indeed.

Back East toward the end of the previous century, in the wake of the Revolutionary War with Britain, New Englanders entered enthusiastically into the business of cutting down trees that had formerly been marked as property of the crown, white pines primarily. In remote areas logging operations *thinned* a square mile at a time. Only on a second go-around had the boys deigned to consider spruce worthy of the bite of a felling axe.

Upstate Vermont was logging country, but the Maine

woods (the District of Maine still officially a part of Massa-
chusetts, though full statehood had been in the wind for
some time now) quickly became the center of activity—over
on the Androscoggin and Kennebec rivers. In short order
tidewater mills began to spring up along the coast, from
Piscataqua to St. Croix.

Getting logs to the mills took white-water men—that
is, individuals who were good on the river, men who cut
logs during winter months and then, with spurs on their
boots, rode logs downstream to the sawyers.

A damn good riverman, now, Beard's father had told
his son more than once, *by Gawd, you can toss a bar of
plain yeller soap into the drink, an' he'll ride them bubbles
to shore. . . .*

Young Bill heard the stories, all of them, from his own
father as well as from others who worked out in the pine
orchards. The lads in the logging woods kept up their own
oral history—and never exaggerated except when they
were of a mind to do so.

Seagull and Calling Owl were fascinated by the horses
owned by the two young men their father had brought into
the lodge—by the horses, yes, and apparently by Raymondo and Guillermo as well. Or perhaps the two young
men and not their animals provided focus for the girls'
attentions.

The American's blue eyes and the yellow-colored hair
on his face gave him the appearance of an owl or a hawk.
Seagull informed Raymondo of the resemblance. And Calling Owl, who liked to stand close to Raymondo, agreed;
Ohlone himself and yet able to command the tongue of his
own childhood. Because of this remembered language, Ray
could tell what the girls were saying even when they
whispered together.

From the point of view of the twins, Beard was an
exotic, and they puzzled as to whether he was in fact
attractive at all. On the other hand, Olivo appeared *human*
enough, and yet the girls clearly did not perceive him as

Ohlone, no matter what heritage he claimed. Oh, they understood well enough what had happened to him. The same fate had nearly claimed their own father. But Pelican Doctor had been able to come back.

Olivo could speak in a language that sounded very much like Hotochrukman—and yet was sufficiently different so that even Pelican Doctor had to listen very carefully in order to understand him. The girls were familiar enough with Spanish, the language Olivo spoke most fluently. They had even learned a bit of English from their father, who had learned from the *Espansh*. And when Beard and Olivo spoke in that tongue, the girls listened carefully.

When the twins were alone inside the lodge, they queried Pelican Doctor at length.

"Father," Seagull asked, "would you be displeased with us if we were to ask the strangers to let us ride on the backs of their *caballos?*"

"Why would you wish to do such a thing, my daughters? Do you mean to ride the horses away and not return to your father's house? Alas, I'll be very lonely if you do such a thing. Then I'll be obliged to kill the two strangers, Bill Beard and Ray Olivo. Well, perhaps our village will have a celebration—perhaps we'll roast the two Californios. When the cooking's finished, I myself will cut off Olivo's arm and—"

"You always say funny things," Calling Owl complained. "First you bring these men into our lodge, and then you pretend we're not supposed to like them."

"That's right," Seagull insisted.

"So," Pelican Doctor laughed. "My twin daughters are now in rebellion against me? No doubt you two wish to marry these strangers and leave your poor old father behind and go to live in separate lodges. But what lodges do Beard and Olivo have? How much money do they have? Where are their strings of dentalium or woodpecker scalps? Shall I let it be known that an Ohlone chief allowed his daughters to be married by foreigners who had not even enough money for a decent bride price?"

"We only asked if it would be all right for us to ride on

the backs of the horses!" Seagull cried out, stamping one foot.

A few miles from Hotochruk, to the south of the redwood canyon where the village was hidden, the furious tides of eons had carved a considerable amphitheaterlike area back into hundred-foot-high, yellow-red sandstone headlands where grebes, gulls, and swallows nested, and at the foot of these cliffs lay an extensive sandy beach which remained dry even at times of high water. The beach was almost perfectly secluded—doubtlessly unsuspected by any casual rider on his way north to the Mission Dolores.

Raymondo discovered the place during the course of a solitary walk, and it was to this spot that he and Bill Beard occasionally retired, whether to bathe under circumstances a bit more private than in the midst of a couple dozen Ohlone men and boys—or simply to be alone, away from the village and the constant chatter of women and children.

In some ways life among the Hotochrukma was beginning to grow wearisome, especially for Beard—but for Raymondo as well, Ohlone though he was. Life as a mission Indian, while hardly attractive, yet provided certain small pleasures which Hotochruk village couldn't match. As for Beard, the Vermonter felt an increasingly intense need to be about some business or another. The slow and in fact utterly casual pace of life among the Ohlones was becoming offensive to his New England soul. Relaxation was fine, but this much relaxation was plain unnatural. Slothfulness was perhaps the deadliest of the deadly sins.

Raymondo and Guillermo tethered their horses where grass grew lushest along the headland and made their way down a steep, faintly visible trail to the beach below. Then the men stripped off their clothing and made a run for the hissing surf hurled in from the deep green depths of the Pacific. They were both skilled swimmers, but a riptide created by projecting headlands and great jagged chunks of broken-away stone provided a genuine task for anyone wishing to work his way out into the deep water.

After testing themselves against the restless swells for perhaps half an hour, the men stroked for shore, back into the cove surrounded by its perpendicular walls of sandstone.

Seagull and Calling Owl were on the beach—holding up articles of clothing and laughing foolishly. Sunlight glinted from the girls' dark hair and tawny limbs. Standing there, with mist rising about them, they seemed almost phantomlike.

Olivo stood neck deep in the surf and demanded that the two young women put his clothing back where they found it and thereupon retire from the amphitheater—in the name of *common sense, good morals, your father's honor, and Christian decency.*

"That won't cut any ice," Beard remarked, at the same time spitting out a mouthful of saltwater. "Not a Christian among the lot of these heathen Hotochrukma devils. . . ."

"Why do you speak of *hielo?*" Raymondo demanded. "Make sense, Bill the Beard! What has frozen water to do with being caught naked by these two highly dangerous females?"

"Precisely everything," Beard replied. "It's a real *bitchkitty.*"

6

Pelican Doctor's Price

"Calling Owl!" Olivo shouted. "You and your sister are to put down our clothing and go away! I order this thing in the name of *Tumas-hachohpa*, the night spirit!"

"The true men of Hotochruk are not concerned for mere women to see them," Calling Owl taunted. "Why are you ashamed?"

"Perhaps these two are deformed," Seagull suggested. "Perhaps they do not even have little horns, in the way of normal men. Or maybe the beard-face, he has two of them. One goes down, the other comes up."

"If it's horns you want, it's horns you'll be getting in a minute or so," Olivo howled. "This child of the mission's coming out no matter what—otherwise I'll break all my teeth from chattering."

"We're not interested in your *horns*," Seagull shouted. "Espansh-men all crazy, I guess. Did you think we wished to scratch your faces—as proper women do to their husbands on the wedding night? No, no. Calling Owl and I, we just want to ride your . . . horses. Is that . . . permitted . . . *Señor Barba*? Mr. Hair-on-the-Face?"

"Pelican Doctor," Calling Owl added, "our father, he said we must ask for your permission. I certainly don't wish to scratch anyone's face. . . ."

The girl did a strange little dance then, spinning about on the wet sand as a wave ebbed. Seagull, more sedate, stood hands-on-hips in a kind of unspoken challenge.

Raymondo Olivo swam toward the beach, emerging from a seethe of foam just behind a large, triangular boulder—which he used to defend his modesty before the twin sisters. Beard also moved toward the girls, wading shoreward but losing his resolve when incoming surges pushed at the small of his back.

"Blue-eyed Bill, you have hair all over your chest and your arms!" Seagull laughed, her voice clearly audible above the hiss of the surf. "Look, sister—the tall one is like a bear that has run through fire and has lost most of his fur—he is different than other men."

"The short one says he is Ohlone, though, a cousin from Saklan, off to the north somewhere," Calling Owl said. "If that is so, then his body won't be covered with hair. I think I'll swim out to take a look for myself. Perhaps he's only an Espansh-man pretending to be one of the people. . . ."

"*Madre de Dios!*" Olivo groaned as a big wave poured in around him, nearly separating him from his hold on the boulder. "These sisters, they're intent upon getting us killed. . . ."

The heavy wave also carried Bill Beard a few feet forward, and when the water receded after driving past him and stinging his eyes, he found it necessary and politic to drop to his knees so as to avoid being exposed.

Just then a flight of ungainly, long-winged pelicans turned inward from over the sea and into the amphitheater where two men and two women were involved in an uncertain, stammering courtship ritual. The birds swooped low to the water, as though unaware of human creatures beneath them, and then with a few beats of their broad wings the gray-white, long-beaked birds sailed gracefully up and over the hundred-foot walls of red-gray sandstone, turned into the wind, and made their way once more out across the reefs and beds of dark green kelp.

On the beach below, meanwhile, Seagull and Calling

Owl had stepped out of their doubled skirts of woven reeds and of deerskin. Holding hands, the pair began to wade into swirling water, moving directly toward the men.

At this point Bill realized someone was standing atop the headland to his right—a powerful man wearing a basket hat. The voyeur was none other than the head chief himself, Pelican Doctor.

The days that followed the embarrassing incident at the beach were relatively difficult—for, in truth, neither Raymondo nor Bill Beard had more than the dimmest notion of what was expected of them. Pelican Doctor said nothing at all—and in no way allowed the men to know he'd ever followed his twin daughters down to the ocean or had stood on the headland above to watch what would transpire—or that he was aware Beard and Olivo were aware he had done so.

That the chief's eyes had caught Beard's own gazing up at him, however, Bill had not the slightest doubt in the world.

Whatever the nature of the game that was being played, Raymondo and Bill were clearly being tested as to mettle and moral character. But the truly maddening complication was that neither man knew the essential rules of the game. Under such circumstances, they had the choices of acting ethically and morally and well, or of fleeing posthaste—and, as it were, never again darkening the entry to Pelican Doctor's lodge. With such givens, Olivo and Beard thought it best to be a bit more distant toward the twins—and yet not even aloofness seemed to bother the ladies. They went on about their business of pursuing the men, just as though nothing at all had happened. Technically, of course, nothing had happened that day— since Bill alerted Raymondo to Pelican Doctor's presence. With the prospect of a most unpleasant death very real in their minds, the men managed to persuade the young women to be so kind as to remain in the water, while they, for their part, made a dash up the sandy beach to their clothing—which garments they managed to climb into most hurriedly.

Seagull and Calling Owl complained loudly and repeatedly—demanding to know why the men thought them both ugly. Was it because the face of neither had been tattooed? At the same time, they insisted, other young men in Hotochruk village believed them to be quite attractive.

How could Bill and Raymondo answer the girls? How indeed?

For Beard, in the act of running nakedly to where his breeches lay on the sand, his long-held fantasy of meeting a beautiful Indian girl off somewhere in the depths of the forest had somehow been fulfilled at the least likely moment and in the least likely manner. Gawddamn it, he even came to realize that he had, without question, fallen in love.

Or had he merely fallen in love with this unlikely realization of his own preconceived and indeed fixed idea?

As for Raymondo, the urgings that had once been directed at Tereza 1002 were apparently now fully set on Calling Owl. She had become his Lady Dulcinea.

"Fate," Raymondo said, scowling, "plays strange tricks on those who set out to be Quixote and Panza."

Was it reasonable to suppose that old Pelican Doctor would be willing to accept the two as sons-in-law? If that were to be the case, then one man would eventually become the head chief of Hotochruk—presuming only that the usual custom concerning the descent of power were followed. More to the point, perhaps: did William Beard, late of the semirepublic of Vermont (land of the Green Mountain Boys) and the free nation known as the United States, wish to acquire an Indian wife? Indeed, Seagull was by now in his thoughts almost constantly—to the point where Beard began to question his own sanity. As attractive as Seagull was, hadn't he enjoyed the favors of many who were certainly no less comely than she? Why was it that he'd never before become so obsessed with the simple *female presence* of a woman? What he felt, he came to realize, hadn't even all that much to do with wanting to bed Seagull, though of course that matter did cross his mind from time to time. *Bed* hardly seemed the appropriate word at all—since he'd virtually reached the point where he couldn't even imagine himself making love to another female, while at the same time he had yet to embrace Seagull in the way of a man and a woman. The thought of someone other than himself making love to her was utterly repugnant, throwing him down into a kind of minor hell when his thoughts verged in that direction. Indeed, when Beard found himself imagining such a thing, he experienced blind rage. Only then was he fully aware of his capacity to commit an act of murder—something quite different than, say, the kind of orchestrated communal mayhem that he'd participated in against the British, there on Lake Champlain.

For a few moments Beard's thoughts drifted eastward across the continent, back to the last time he'd seen Christie. She'd stood there in front of the church that Sunday morning, Tom Ebersoll standing beside her, good old Tom, skinny and solemn just as he'd always been. Beard noted a certain glow to Christie's complexion, and he wondered idly if she'd gotten herself into a family way once more.

Given her druthers, and she'd breed a new nation. . . .

Christie, demure and proper. Then she'd winked at him, opened her lips slightly, and twice touched the tip of her tongue to her upper lip.

That evening he met her in the close spring darkness, there in the old secret place, and they held one another desperately and indulged in memories and said a great many things that neither truly meant. Their kisses denoted both greeting and farewell. . . .

That memory, and the others—things that might as well have happened to someone else.

Beard dismissed the past, and the image of the present delineated itself within his mind.

Seagull.

Beard grinned. No one who didn't know the twins fairly well would even have been able to tell them apart, yet he and Raymondo knew them clearly enough—his desire was all toward Seagull, while Raymondo's was toward Calling Owl.

What in Gawd's name had come over the two of them? What dark and inexplicable secrets lay coded deep in the blood and fibers of the human male that brought about so sudden and total an alteration? They could only hope that, somehow, a parallel magnetism had worked its magic upon the psyches of the women toward whom the not altogether reformed horse thieves were drawn.

In truth, Beard had always supposed that ultimately, when his time of adventuring was past, he'd return to New England and there discover and pay court to the eldest daughter of a good family in some such town as Lowell or Orleans—a woman, perhaps, already past the first flower of beauty and hence regarded as something of an old maid. A more sedate version of Christie, so to speak. A young widow might be another possibility. With Ebersoll in the grave. . . . Under such circumstances, Bill reasoned, his offer of marriage could hardly be turned down—and the union itself was certain to prove durable.

For this reason, the turmoil that now pervaded his guts left him astonished, dumbfounded, and (so it seemed) virtually helpless.

Two final considerations: what would it be like to have half an Indian village for in-laws? And what would be the response on the part of his own kin in Vermont, on that inevitable day when he showed up with an Ohlone wife in tow?

At length Pelican Doctor returned the weapons and informed Beard and Olivo that they were free to leave the village and return to their own people, if they wished to do so.

"The band of horses," the chief added, "are yours—and so you are free to do with the medicine dogs as you yourselves see fit. No doubt you stole them from one of the haciendas. . . ."

Bill glanced at Raymondo. Doubt was written all over the smaller man's swarthy face.

"We have been very . . . comfortable here among your people, Pelican Doctor," Raymondo said. "Do you now wish for us to leave you?"

The chief's expression was impassive.

"I thought perhaps you wished to go," he replied. "If that's the case, then neither I nor my daughters . . . warriors . . . will attempt to prevent you. Now that you have your guns back, of course, you can shoot us if we try to stop you."

"Pelican Doctor and his men also have firearms." Raymondo grinned. "If we fired, then you would fire back."

"Maybe so. Well, now you're free to do as you wish."

The chief withdrew his stone pipe from its sealskin case, tamped into the bowl a quantity of native tobacco, and utilized a glowing stick from the firepit to light the mixture. He gestured to the earth and to the sea and to the heavens, rotating the long-stemmed pipe completely about so as to indicate the yearly seasons, and then sipped at the smoke. This preliminary ritual completed, Pelican Doctor passed the pipe to Raymondo, who repeated the chief's actions and proceeded to pass the pipe to Bill.

When Beard also had tasted the strong tobacco smoke, he handed the pipe back to Pelican Doctor.

The chief appeared reflective. He also appeared quite old.

"You have been my sons for a time, but now, *P'an' tanzhi*, the time is past. It is a new world for all of us."

Beard nodded.

"Raymondo and I . . . wish to remain for a time with Pelican Doctor and his people," Bill said, glancing quickly at Raymondo to be certain his friend agreed with what he'd uttered. The look in Raymondo's eyes was almost one of relief.

The chief studied both men, sipped once again of the smoke, and nodded.

"It is good," he said.

Olivo nodded, glanced at Beard.

"Do you find my daughters pleasing?" Pelican Doctor asked. "I believe it's nearly time for them to take husbands. They have minds of their own, however, and I wish to do nothing to force them into marriages that don't make them happy."

On an occasion when nearly the entire village of Hotochruk was to troop down to where the creek passed through a small lagoonlike swamp and then out into the Pacific Ocean, the Ohlones intent upon gathering mussels and clams and netting rock cod, Pelican Doctor invited Raymondo and Bill to come along. The walk would be good, he insisted, inasmuch as the *Whitemen* spent far too much time on horseback. Furthermore, the chief assured them, they would be amazed at the skill of the young men who dived down, short fishing spears in hand, to pry loose the big red-and-silver-shelled oysters called *avalones*, or *abalones*, as the Spanish pronounced the word.

Since Padre Orontes had first showed Beard these shells and told him their name, he'd suspected the native term for the Costanoan people, *Ohlones*, was nothing more than a variant of the term. *Those who gather shellfish*. Bill could only presume the native peoples had somehow readopted their own word, which had been appropriated by the Spanish and used as a sort of alternate designation.

They accompanied Pelican Doctor, who, rather than lead his people, preferred to walk along at the rear of the band. The chief carried his flintlock rifle, a piece of Spanish manufacture, while at the head of the procession were several men with either horse pistols or fusees. The Hotochrukma were, as a matter of fact, relatively well-armed and quite able to defend themselves, should a band of Leather Jackets unexpectedly make an appearance. Had it been possible for the chief to commandeer a full man o' war, Bill mused, he'd have had no hesitancy in doing so.

Admiral Pelican Doctor, in Napoleonic uniform but sporting a basket hat, wearing a combat sword and a brace of pistols, standing on the prow and staring through an eyeglass toward an approaching British fleet . . .

Caught up with the general spirit of the moment, Seagull and Calling Owl moved off ahead in the company of several young women their own age. Pelican Doctor clucked his tongue and muttered something about the changeable natures and whims of young women.

The five-mile venture to the ocean went slowly, with numerous stops along the stream and with bands of children setting off through the redwoods as though on rival war parties, much to the chagrin of their mothers. The hour was still well before noon when the band arrived, however. Mid-August though it was, a steady offshore wind was riding in over booming waves of the incoming tide, and Pelican Doctor gave directions that a fire be made.

Children quickly mobilized to gather driftwood from high up on the beach, some searching for dry twigs or sprays of dead bush lupines, while others sought heftier chunks—limbs and knots that earlier tides had hurled up the littoral. With leaves and twigs placed in a small mound within a scooped-out cavity in the sand, Pelican Doctor dropped to his knees, using flint and steel as dexterously as any man alive, and within a short time he had a considerable blaze laughing in the wind.

Only Pelican Doctor and Raymondo and Bill, as well as the younger children and a few of their mothers, remained close about the fire, however, for a majority of the Ohlones were soon scattered up and down the beaches or had vanished beyond the headlands to the north and to the south. Pelican Doctor nodded, seeming at that moment not only human but almost disgustingly so—the grandfather of his people, fully aware of his authority and also of its limitations, and greatly pleased with the brood of offspring who had come into being during his tenure as leader of the Hotochrukma.

"Some who reach my age," the chief confided, "think

only of acquiring younger wives, for such men imagine they
will need someone to take care of them when they become
feeble. Me, I do not think in that way. In the first place, I
have no intention of ever growing feeble—though one
should not speak in such a fashion for fear that Old Coyote
himself may be listening. Nonetheless, I believe that
Hummingbird will outsmart Coyote in this case—for when
I feel old age beginning to come on me, I am going to go to
the Santa Cruz Mission and murder all the priests there. No
doubt the soldiers will shoot me, but that will be all right.
In this way my people will be required to choose another
leader, a younger man. . . . There is one more reason
also—that is, one more reason why I'm not interested in
taking a new wife. She who was my mate wouldn't be
pleased, you see. She waits for me in Other Side Camp.
When she died, I wished to follow her into the Spirit
World, but she came to me in a dream and told me that I
was to remain with the people, since they needed me. She
told me that we would both have to be patient."

Beard and Olivo were equally startled by this singular
outpouring from one who was generally so taciturn.

"Do you believe men our age," Raymondo began,
pointing to himself and to Bill as well, "ought to consider
taking wives? It seems to me that if we're to live among
your people, Pelican Doctor, then we ought to be allowed
to have families. . . ."

Pelican Doctor kneeled beside the fire, tossed a couple
more chunks of driftwood into the flames, and stood up
once again. He crossed his arms, pursed his lips, and looked
quite solemn.

"I believe you're right, Señor Olivo," he said. "Does
the man with the hairy face agree with you?"

"I'm also of that opinion," Bill Beard replied.

"Have you two found women, then, who appeal to
you?"

Suddenly Beard felt quite foolish. The old reprobate
had been leading them on all the while. . . .

"Yes, as a matter of fact," Bill replied, "we have—your
very own *hijas*, Seagull and Calling Owl."

Pelican Doctor stared out across the rolling surf, pointed to a low-flying stream of gulls that suddenly veered upward, taking the air and sailing off toward a reef half a mile from shore.

"It will be good," the chief said. "What have my friends Olivo and Beard to offer me as bride prices? It is only just that the daughters of the head chief should command high prices, for in that way their status within the village is assured. Do you understand what I'm saying to you?"

"*Sí, sí*, yes, we *comprendemos*," Raymondo agreed.

"The horses," Bill said quickly. "Raymondo and I will present you with all our horses."

"I speak to you of a bride price," the chief answered, "because I already know what is in my daughters' hearts. They made their choice at least a moon ago, and since then they have had to wait for you. I want my daughters to be happy, and that's why I'm willing to have you men for son-in-laws. I would have preferred young men of our own village or perhaps from some other Ohlone village, but that's another matter. What I must tell you now, however, will not make your hearts glad."

"You demand more than the horses?" Olivo asked. "Your daughters are indeed beautiful, but—"

"Is not that," Pelican Doctor replied. "What would I do with horses? What would my people do? We have no need of medicine dogs, though I admit they are fine creatures. No, it's a different kind of price that I would have you pay me. You must keep the horses. I think perhaps you can sell some of them and use the Spanish money to purchase firearms and ammunition. That would be a bride price I might share with my people—for one day, almost certainly, the Leather Jackets will begin to think that now they are strong enough to overpower Pelican Doctor and the Hotochrukma. We need many more pistols, I think, and a large quantity of gunpowder. If you'll bring me these things, you may have my daughters to marriage."

> *Dancing on the brink of the world* . . .
>
> *I dream of you,*
> *I dream of you jumping,*
> *Rabbit, jack rabbit, and quail* . . .
>
> *Dancing on the brink of the world.* . . .

Beard and Olivo found the girls at the mouth of a small cove beyond a protruding sandstone headland, for to this spot the women had retired after filling their woven baskets with mussels.

At first they hid from the men and refused to answer when both Bill and Raymondo called out their names; but when the men pretended that they would go away, the girls darted out from the willow and lupine and azalea thickets where they'd taken refuge.

"Come with me," Beard said to Seagull—and, sensing the serious tone to his voice, she followed along and was soon walking no more than half a pace behind.

"*Hileu ma tanim*, where are you going, Billium Beard? Are you angry with both Calling Owl and Raymondo—and so do not wish to be near them?"

Bill stopped then and turned to Seagull, placed his hands on her shoulders—forced himself not to stare at the beautifully formed, dark-nippled, bare breasts.

She gazed up at him, her sensuously full lips slightly parted.

"Something is wrong, then?" she asked, her voice now quite serious.

"I'm not certain," Bill replied. "Seagull, I think you know how I feel about you. Well, I've asked Pelican Doctor if I might have you for my wife."

She blushed now and lowered her eyes.

"And he agreed," the Vermonter continued, "if I could bring him an appropriate bride price."

"Did Raymondo ask also, or . . . ?"

"Raymondo asked for the hand of Calling Owl."

Seagull looked up, her mouth now taken with the hint of a smile.

"We offered our horses, Seagull, but your father insists that he wants guns and gunpowder instead, and I can see no way for us to—"

"Will the Mexican Espansh not sell these weapons to you?" Seagull asked. "You have a pale skin, just like some of them. In Villa de Branciforte, there the men have such weapons for sale. My father has told me that often. The Espansh will not sell such things to Indian people, but they will sell them to you, Bill Beard."

"I don't know. Raymondo and I—well, we sort of stole our horses from the mission at San José. If we now go in to Branciforte, perhaps the Leather Jackets will arrest us and hang us. . . ."

"Then you must not do such a thing. Surely there is another way. Pelican Doctor has spoken of the place called Monte-rey, far off to the south. You and Raymondo could ride there on your horses."

"Perhaps, perhaps. But what if we're unable to do what you suggest? I love you, Seagull. Would you be willing to leave Hotochruk and go away with me? Calling Owl and Raymondo also, of course. We could go north, north to where the British have cities and trading posts. Ray and I could trap furs and become very wealthy, and after that—"

"No," Seagull replied. "My sister and I, we can never leave our father. How could we leave the one who raised us after our mother died? You and Raymondo must stay here. Calling Owl and I will beg our father to change his mind. He and the other men already have Espansh weapons, and yet they do not use them. We will show you how to collect money shells—or perhaps you will be able to sell your horses to the people at Kino-te or at Matala-n. Do you really love me, Bill Beard? Tell me the truth now. I will gladly lie down with you no matter what you say—I have hardly been able to think of anything else for a long while now, even though I have never before lain with a man and am not really certain what I must do. . . ."

He pressed his lips to hers, at the same time wondering if she'd understand. Yes, Ohlone women kissed their lovers, but only in private. . . . He was willing to rub noses instead—that or just hold on to her and press his body to hers. Such an embrace, all things considered, would be quite satisfactory.

"Calling Owl told me about this thing," she whispered afterward. "Raymondo kissed her several days ago. I was afraid you didn't wish to kiss me, Bill Beard. But maybe it's just that you're more timid than your friend is."

That damnable Olivo—why didn't he tell me he was meeting secretly with Calling Owl?

7

The Idea of Shingles

Bill Beard and Raymondo Olivo talked at some length, and ultimately decided to make an attempt to sell their horses at Villa de Branciforte—or, if necessary, at Monterey. Together they'd drive their entire remuda southward, staying away from the trail that led along the headlands and sticking, insofar as possible, to the crests of the mountains. According to Pelican Doctor, they'd be able to remain under the cover of forest growth, whether of redwood and fir or of oaks and the rapidly growing stands of Australian blue gums, seeds of which had been planted in areas where fire had scorched the hillsides or where native liveoak and black oak had been felled in order to secure fuel, or where Monterey pines and some immature redwoods had been taken down to produce structural timbers.

The plan was this: to establish a brush corral perhaps five miles or so from Branciforte and to take in two or three horses at a time. Olivo would stay behind in the forest to tend the animals. Even if a reward were posted for the two men, considerable time had passed, and owing to the American's long hair, much fuller beard, and buckskin apparel, Bill now appeared quite different, or so he supposed, than had been the case when he'd shown up at the Godly establishment in San José. Alone, there would be little reason for anyone to associate him with a Vermonter named Benjamin Barrington, a man undoubtedly charged with assisting in the kidnapping of Fray Orontes. In any case, with Raymondo left behind, Bill would attempt to drive a bargain for the horses—to convert the animals, in other words, into a few of the weapons Pelican Doctor wanted as a bride price.

Beard already supposed he knew what the possibilities for success were. None. In this land, firearms were doubtlessly at a premium—available, but not in exchange for such goods as the partners had to offer.

Affecting as casual a posture as possible and trailing four ponies behind his own, Bill made his way into Branciforte. The village into which he rode was busy at midmorning, and as a matter of fact no one paid him the slightest degree of attention. The inhabitants of this more-or-less outlaw settlement, as Beard was to learn directly, were of various sorts—mostly Mexican-Spanish, but a few others who, like himself, had jumped ship and found their way to this strange place: Dutchmen, a handful of Hidalgos, Britishers, and even a pair of surly Russians.

Bill utilized only Spanish, in this way taking care to hide his Yankeehood. That he was no Californio, however, was not to be hidden, for his accent precluded such a possibility. While he was hardly a master of *Español*, his ability with the tongue was sufficient, as he soon discovered—for in this minuscule city of irregulars, a cacophony of variant pronunciations was virtually the rule.

The master of the livery stable was a scar-faced, one-eyed Spaniard who was at the same time both highly suspicious and extremely garrulous—so that the latter attribute effectively canceled the former.

For his own part, Bill Beard spoke no more than was necessary.

"*Dinero? Dinero e plata? Quiero que comprar los caballos.*"

The one-eyed Spaniard squinted and displayed a broken-toothed grin. Bill wondered momentarily about how the man had lost his eye—for Beard could almost see him at some point in his life aboard a Spanish man o' war, yes, and engaged in hand-to-hand combat. Bill could almost see the dagger in a Dutchman's hand as the blade. . . .

The livery master offered a price, and Bill nearly accepted without attempting to bargain. Realizing such an action might be deemed suspicious, however, he set about haggling with the man.

One-Eye nodded, muttered a few words, and then made more careful inspection of the horses. Directly a somewhat higher price was offered.

Again Bill did not accept—insisting on twice the amount.

The liveryman turned his head, spat, and cursed; Beard, meanwhile, made particular note of the long, adze-marked beams which held up the roof of the livery. The structural members were redwood; the texture and uniform color were proof certain. In the New Englander's mind's eye danced a vision of whole mansions built entirely of redwood, with unpainted exteriors slowly turning silver-white under the influence of rains and mists as years went by—just as was the case with broken segments of the wood lying beside the creek near Hotochruk village.

The one-eyed man made a counter offer, and Bill decided against pushing his luck further.

Dinero in hand, Beard rode back toward the encampment where Raymondo Olivo awaited his return. The day was beautiful indeed, with midsummer warmth penetrating the fogs that seemed perpetually to hang off the coast, and the sky overhead a faultless blue.

As Bill worked his way along the trail, upslope from the little valley that contained Branciforte, a silent explosion went up in the midst of a clearing ahead of him—and his pony startled, going sidestep, nearly throwing the rider.

Three California condors took flight, climbing the air in a frenzy—and Beard was stunned by the massive size of these birds, the power of their wings. Never before had he seen their kind at so close a distance. Indeed, on numerous occasions Raymondo had been obliged to point out to him which long-winged birds, high up and riding invisible currents of wind, were turkey vultures, and which were hawks or eagles, and which were actually the king birds, reverenced by some of the Indian peoples as either gods or as the spirits of dead relatives, incarnate in beak and pinion feather.

Once Bill arrived at the encampment, he and Raymondo congratulated one another, enjoyed dinner and the flask of wine he'd purchased in Branciforte, and discussed prospects. Among other matters, Bill spoke of the eventual building of an all-purpose mill such as those he'd seen in New England, one with a great circular saw driven by belt from a waterwheel, or even one powered by steam. With such modern equipment, Bill asserted, lumber could be manufactured for export—to such places as South America or the Sandwich Islands. If redwoods grew nowhere but in California, and if the quality of the material (as yet undetermined) was as Beard hoped might be the case, he could even envision exporting lumber to New York or Boston or London or Lisbon. . . .

Olivo agreed with most of what his Yankee partner said, but Bill had the feeling that Raymondo believed his friend's sanity somewhat suspect.

"True, we have sold some of our horses," Raymondo cautioned, "but all the rest of this is like a dream. One must be careful not to confuse dreams with those things which are real, Guillermo. It was such a fault that so often misled Don Quixote. . . ."

Bill laughed, nodded, and took another pull from the flask.

Early the following morning, Beard was once again on his way, this time with an additional four ponies. Where the condors startled his horse the previous day, however, he found nothing but some bits of deerhide and bone. The big birds, or so he gathered, had been joined at the feeding by coyotes and wolves and no doubt carrion crows, vultures, and possums as well. Oddly enough, hardly a trace of odor remained.

Trading went well that day in Branciforte, and with his mission successfully completed, Bill rode back to the brush corral, bearing with him one more flask of wine as well as a box of Panamanian cigars.

After no more than a drink or two, he and Raymondo concluded that the time had clearly come for them to move their operations elsewhere—to a larger and more potentially profitable market. The friends ate a good dinner of venison and wild parsnip, drank wine, and capped the feast off with a cigar apiece. Thereupon they spent some time in discussion of the brazen barber's basin which Don Quixote mistakenly supposed to be the fabled helmet of the warrior Mambrino—the very helmet of invincibility. Bill argued that the fable's author intended his readers to understand that the object was without any magic whatsoever, while Raymondo (having drunk perhaps a bit more wine) insisted that appearances are indeed deceiving and that, as events depicted later in the book would show, that very brazen pot, however utilitarian its supposed function, yet had about it *glamor* sufficient to allow Don Quixote to achieve a degree of greatness.

With this purely hypothetical issue still unresolved, they both fell asleep in mid-argument and awoke only when the sun had already rimmed the canyon they were camped in.

They took a light breakfast and set out southward, avoiding several small settlements. With the remainder of their horses trailing behind them, Raymondo and Bill rode toward Monterey, the latter in the guise of a free trapper, and the former in the role of an Indian varlet—for in such an arrangement, they'd concluded, a minimum of suspicion would be aroused.

"It's just as I have always said, Sancho." Beard laughed. "In this world, those who are both tall and who have bearded faces are the natural leaders."

Olivo shrugged.

"From the beginning," he replied, "Don Quixote was the crazy one. In any case, the length of one's legs does not determine the quality of that which resides within the skull.

Lead on—but don't expect me to follow you into any battles against giants with fans for arms. . . ."

Early the second day of their venture, they arrived at the small capital city of Monterey, and luck, as matters turned out, was with them. Within sight of the actual residence of Governor Pablo Vicente de Sola, they were able to receive a considerably higher price for the remaining animals than they'd expected. Apparently the one-eyed Spaniard in Branciforte had outbargained the Yankee after all.

The Monterey stables were owned by an eccentric Frenchman by the name of Jean Paul Martin, one who also attended a hardware establishment and had weapons for sale, as well as a wide variety of tools, some locally fabricated and some of Mexican manufacture. Furthermore (as the partners soon began to realize) he was a man of considerable reputation and wealth. That he should be personally attending a mercantile establishment, apparently, was more a matter of whim than necessity.

Expressing interest in a pistol Martin had on display, Bill took the opportunity to examine several weapons, both handguns and flintlock rifles. At length he made Martin an offer on three used horse pistols and a French rifle, as well as a quantity of both lead and gunpowder.

Bill gestured toward Raymondo.

"Señor Hermes and I," Beard told Martin, "we are going to set up a shingle mill. Do you think perhaps we will find a ready market for redwood roofing?"

"*Eh bien*, that explains it. Why you need the tools— but what of the firearms, *les fusils?* Monsieur Beard, what am I to think of these?"

"Indians and grizzlies," Bill replied, endeavoring to maintain a straight face. "We presume it will be necessary to defend our holdings."

"The Indians, they are tame—all but one village, and that is said to be somewhere in the mountains to the north of Santa Cruz. Or do you intend to go south, into the Ventanas? Or north, into the mountains beyond Bahía del

San Francisco? Yet the grizzly bears, *enfant de garce*, that is another matter. Beard and Hermes? I think perhaps you two are highwaymen who have now decided to resort to honest work. Well, all the better, *très bien!*"

Bill laughed. "Jean Paul Martin, you gabble on like some hysterical old woman with bad teeth and a big belly. Answer my question, señor. Do you believe we'll find a ready market if we bring in ox carts piled high with shingles cut from redwood?"

The Frenchman's face grew reflective.

"That kind of wood, it is said to be not very strong. That is why most do not cut structural beams from it. Also it does not burn very well. Maybe for shingles it is a good idea. Perhaps I will sell these shingles for you. Bring me enough shingles, and we sell them everywhere, *tout le monde.*"

After some discussion and even the signing of a makeshift document or two, the latter signifying Martin's expressed mercantile interest in the redwood project (in exchange for which letters of credit were to be issued in behalf of Señors Beard and Hermes), the men shook hands all around.

Business completed, Bill and Raymondo were soon on the road northward—well-armed and trailing a two-wheeled drayage cart drawn by a single docile ox which was, as the saying goes, somewhat long in the tooth. Among other items, the cargo consisted of hatchets, three splitting mauls, a matched pair of twelve-inch felling axes, steel wedges, and a whipsaw, as well as several sacks of rolled oats, wheat, and corn. Such were not, of course, among those things that Pelican Doctor had specified as a bride price. But with them, as Raymondo and Bill schemed, the partners would be able to earn the specified bride prices several times over.

"In moments of economic difficulty," William Beard made pronouncement, "there's nothing like good old-fashioned Yankee enterprise."

"We have talked much, Sancho," Raymondo Olivo said, his face a mask of doubt, "but now we'll be obliged to produce that of which we have spoken so glibly. The redwood trees, they are all very large. It will take us a long while to turn them into shingles. . . ."

They avoided Santa Cruz and Villa de Branciforte, circling inland and then proceeding northward through the mountains, not returning to the coast road until they'd passed beyond the amphitheaterlike cove where Pelican Doctor had spied down upon two naked swimmers being harassed by pair of Hotochrukma twins.

Raymondo and Bill tethered their ox where the draft animal might drink and graze a bit while still in its traces, and then they rode out onto the headland above the cove—a distance of no more than a couple hundred yards. The men stared down to the enclosed beach. Great green-black waves glinted intense sunlight and then crashed headlong into ragged, mussel and barnacle-encrusted boulders at the base of the cliffs, sending white spume high into the air. The waves, where unimpeded, rolled far up onto the sand before losing momentum and then draining back into the faces of other waves that followed in more or less regular measure.

Birds of the coast, drifting idly and apparently utterly unconcerned with the violent confrontation of wave and rock, dipped their black-tipped wings in sunlight and came riding up the air currents to inspect humans on horseback astride the headland.

Raymondo shook his head.

"This is where it began," he said. "Well, perhaps much earlier. And yet, here on the beach, here on the beach was where our lot was cast. The dice, the dice! Just such a pair of numbers came up, Señor Beard, and you and I were caught. No longer was there any escape for us."

"Caught by love," Bill mused. "Yes, I suppose we were at that. You and I pursue our own versions of Dulcinea, *hermano*, and yet the ladies are truly beautiful, is that not so? Speak the truth, Raymondo."

"Like all males, we think only with what hangs between our legs. We see these sisters and suppose them pretty—no, not pretty, but rather the most desirable women in all the world—and so we are caught. It has ever been thus in matters of men and women. Indeed, do I not have scars on my back that illustrate this elemental truth?"

"Philosophy and ethics," Bill grinned. "You're back to being Quixote once more."

"Was there ever any doubt?" Raymondo asked as he turned his horse about and pressed his heels into the creature's ribs.

Pelican Doctor took the weapons and ammunition the partners brought him *on account*—and of course Raymondo and Bill both knew all along that three pistols and a French rifle wouldn't satisfy the Ohlone chief's desire to be fully armed in the event of a substantial attack by Leather Jackets.

As to a presumed lack of wisdom in acquiring a drayage wagon and the various tools, however, Pelican Doctor could merely shake his head and mutter something about how it was that young men in love usually did not display such patience.

When Bill explained that he and Raymondo fully intended to transform the axes and hatchets and saw into additional weaponry, the chief stared impassively at his prospective son-in-laws.

"That will be powerful magic, then," Pelican Doctor remarked. "Those who would marry my daughters must explain this wonder to the girls. Then perhaps the girls will be willing to tell me what they have learned. Right now you two have caused my head to hurt."

Thereupon Pelican Doctor turned away and vanished into his lodge. Clearly, he wished no further company at the present time.

Seagull and Calling Owl also expressed puzzlement that afternoon as the two couples, along with half a dozen children who'd been put temporarily into the twins' care, walked upstream along the creek to where the stone face of one of the Ancient Ones stared out from beside a now diminished waterfall.

Seagull and Bill left Raymondo and Calling Owl to tend the children, and the man and the woman worked their way around the falls and into a narrow, sun- and shadow-filled ravine above—a place that seemed entirely remote from the rest of the world.

"What will you do with these things you've traded for?" Seagull asked.

"We'll use them to cut up the trunks of trees."

"Those steel axes look very clumsy to me. Even if one could learn to use them, they wouldn't do so fine a job as the stone-headed axes my people have always used to work on pieces of wood. Do the Espansh men use such tools? Yes, that's where you got them. And what is the other piece of metal for—the long jagged one with the handles on it?"

"That is a cross-cut saw. Raymondo and I will use it to cut logs into short sections."

"Why would you wish to do that?"

"Well . . . this won't make a great deal of sense to you, Gull, but we'll be cutting logs and then splitting them into little thin sections—shingles. They're used to put on the roofs of some of the Californios' lodges, those that don't use tiles. If shingles are overlapped just right, the rain runs off—can't get into the inside. Same idea as using thatch on the lodges in the village, actually."

"If thatch works, then why go to all the trouble of cutting up these . . . shingles?"

Bill nodded, winked, and kissed Seagull on the bare, brown skin of her shoulder.

"Raymondo and I will be able to sell the shingles to the Californios, and they will use them to keep the rain out of their houses. If we can make enough shingles, we can sell them to the men who come in the sailing ships—and they'll take them to places halfway around the world. Raymondo and I'll become wealthy, and then we'll be able to buy your father as many weapons as he would like to have."

Seagull stared into Beard's eyes as if to make determination whether he was simply playing with words—making up a great, complicated lie with which to amuse himself—or whether, indeed, something had gone wrong inside his skull.

"The wood of the redwood is unusual," Bill continued. "The trees resist fire—that's why so often the old ones have black scars, and yet they live through the times of fire and get to be very old and very big. The wood's much less heavy than that of oak or fir. Furthermore, it doesn't rot the way other wood does—I think there must be some substance in it that acts like a poison to mold and even to insects. One could build whole houses with it. . . ."

"There are many logs lying on the ground, trees that the winds have uprooted. So you and Raymondo will cut these up and then carry your *shingles* in the cart that your ox pulls along? In this way you'll take your shingles into Branciforte or Santa Cruz and sell them to the Espansh people?"

Bill could see that Seagull was on the verge of comprehending the essential idea of Whiteman's commerce—not so different, after all, from the trading sessions that various Ohlone groups engaged in. But he could also see that something else was about to explode in her mind. He waited for that further question:

"It may take several winters, but what happens when there are no more fallen trees to cut up? What will you do then, Bill Beard?"

"Start cutting down the live ones," he answered. "Just the smaller trees, of course—since Pelican Doctor says the spirits of the dead live in many of the big redwoods."

"Besides," Seagull said quickly, her face brightening, "no one could cut down the larger trees. Redwoods are too big for that. If they ever did fall, the earth itself would shake. Pelican Doctor says that when the ground trembles, it's because some huge old tree has fallen."

"In any case," Bill continued, "this is one way in which Raymondo and I can get the weapons your father has asked for, and it's also a way in which we can become fairly wealthy—though in all likelihood, after a few years, we'll end up leaving Hotochruk—you and I and Raymondo and

Calling Owl, I mean. A time will come, Seagull, when your people and your father's people will also be obliged to live as the Whitemen live. Perhaps the warriors will herd cattle or work as loggers. The Whiteman has a thirst for logs, so to speak. No, no, I understand—it's not possible for one to swallow a log. Right. But that's not what I mean. You mustn't be so damned literal in your thinking, Gull. The Whites build houses, and for that reason they need such things as boards and shingles. The Mexican Spanish see the forests on the mountains around them, but they don't see the utility of these trees. You must understand—I didn't come from either Spain or Mexico. Hell no, I'm a Yankee, an American. We understand about cutting trees down. In Vermont, it was necessary to clear the forests from the land so that we could plant crops—clear the land in order to survive. It'll be that way here too, eventually. You'll see. My people, the *Americans*, they'll come here one day—and this land will be part of the *United States of America*."

Seagull looked distinctly troubled.

"Where is this *Vermont*?" she asked.

Bill Beard smiled, nodded.

"It's . . . well, it's far off, far off in the direction where the sun rises. It's near the Great Water far to the east. I came here in one of the sailing ships you've seen out to sea—you told me you'd seen such a ship. . . ."

"I don't like your vision of the future," Seagull said. "Besides, my people will never agree to dress as the Whitemen, live in square houses made out of dried mud, like the Espansh. No, the Hotochrukma will continue as they have always been. Only perhaps my father will decide to kill all the Mexican-Espansh as soon as he has enough guns. That would be good—for then both Grizzly and Condor would approve of the killings."

"But I'm White, aren't I?"

"No longer," Seagull insisted. "When you were taken prisoner by Pelican Doctor and his men, you became one of the people. I don't wish you to leave . . . us . . . , Billy Beard."

He gazed into Seagull's eyes for a long moment, and

there he saw the gleamings of desire—desire, yes, but a fear of loss as well. He drew her to him, tilted her head back, and kissed her full on the mouth.

A moment later she burst out laughing—not, he had to admit, precisely the response he'd hoped for.

No true Vermont Yankee likes having his best efforts at lovemaking laughed at.

"Do that again, Bill-Beard," she whispered, her eyes closed and her lips slightly parted.

A true cavalier, he reflected, was oath-bound to the performance of whatever it was that his lady desired. His musings, however, didn't last long—for Seagull's mouth was now fairly glued to his, and indeed he felt as though caught up in the tentacles of a pleasure-producing octopus. At that moment Bill was certain Seagull had at least eight arms.

One of her numerous hands found its way to the spot just between his legs, and he groaned softly as she squeezed.

"You don't wish to wait?" he asked.

"Wait for what? Blue-eyed men are crazy, maybe."

"For our marriage, Seagull. You mustn't let me talk you into anything you don't want to do."

She was still kissing him, but her fingers were busily unlacing his breeches.

"Time for you to show me your little horn, your *pauoi.* . . ."

Then they were rolling together in a texture of sunlight and shade, and all about them rose music of bird song and gurgling water as the stream moved off westward toward the brink of what Pelican Doctor himself called Stone Face Falls.

Not like a . . . Vermont woman. Seagull, she's a child, and yet without shame, shameless, innocent, utterly immodest, free, perhaps I will learn freedom from this woman. . . .

When the time of passion was over, they clung together, allowing their breathing to steady, and their bodies dripped with perspiration. Bill lay on his back with Seagull crouched on top of him, her head resting against his chin, and her long, black hair draped over both of them. A kingfisher screamed angrily as it flashed through his vision, a blue dart whose voice left an afterglow of red as his awareness lapsed into a brief and contented sleep. In some sense or another, they were Adam and Eve, he and she, and the world was all before them.

8

The Chief's Vision

As in all confrontations, whether human or animal, a ritual show of force or of justified authority will often accomplish far more than actual combat. In the long run, if Raymondo and Bill were successful, the entire nature of life in these *barrancas* where the Ohlones were presently master would be altered irreversibly. Bill Beard believed it true that he understood this unfortunate reality far more certainly than did Raymondo Olivo, even though his friend had seen all too vividly in the course of his own life the impact Spanish-Catholic civilization had wrought upon the Ohlones—and upon every other native group with whom they'd come into contact. Ultimately, the short bow and the spear were simply no match for Leather Jacket cavalry equipped with swords of fine steel or pistols and rifles—even if the Indian peoples occasionally displayed superior tactics and bravery.

Just as the Spanish had subdued the land of Mexico, so, as a consequence, the Mexican Spanish, primarily Indian in blood but Spanish in cultural legacy, subdued the Indians along the coast. A new people had already emerged, the *Gente de Razón*, Californios.

Still, Spanish presence in California was a matter of long standing, its overall impact relatively slight from the point of view of those Indians who continued to enjoy their savage, primal heritage—by means of having withdrawn to those remote areas that were at present of no utilitarian value either to the Church or the government. Civilized population in the land was relatively small. Indeed, the Indian peoples were numerous by contrast.

Raymondo, even with his passion for learning, hadn't seen such places as Bangor, Portland, Boston, New Haven, or New York. As a consequence, he couldn't fully realize the amazing transformations that Yankee industry could bring about within a short span of years.

While it was certainly true that Bill himself was presently a citizen of the village of Hotochruk, he was nonetheless an American at heart, a man with Yankee visions. Part of what he could see down the long path of the future was that this land of California would make an admirable addition to the new and growing and thriving nation to which he owed primary allegiance. Had the United States not twice defeated the mighty British? What threat, then, could Spain pose? Or Mexico itself, should that nation cast off the Spanish? Yankee ships plied the oceans of the world, and it would be no great military matter for a constellation of American frigates to take Monterey and so lay claim to the fair land of California.

William Beard was hardly the first to envision a federation of American states which spanned the North American continent, for was that not Thomas Jefferson's great dream? To such an end the nation acquired the Louisiana Purchase. Ten years had now passed since Lewis and Clark, at Jefferson's direction, traversed the great North American interior and thereby enforced the United States' claim to the land known as Oregon.

Bill could see dairy farms, water mills, factories capable of producing such necessary goods as firearms, clothing, books, lumber. . . .

Though natural attrition over the years had brought down a considerably supply of redwood logs sufficient to their purpose, Raymondo and Bill concluded that they needed to impress Pelican Doctor and his people, for a number of the warriors had begun to view the two outsiders as madmen, crazy ones who'd spent too much time in the moonlight.

For reasons of wishing to be deemed both rational and capable, then, Olivo and Beard made a show of felling a redwood of considerable size, a tree perhaps four feet in diameter and a hundred and fifty feet or so in height. Though quite modest when contrasted to some of the titanic redwoods, nonetheless this tree was greater in girth and taller than any tree Bill had ever worked on in the forests of Vermont or New Hampshire. Raymondo hadn't used a felling axe before, and so this first minor giant amounted to a kind of practical training ground for the both of them. The task wasn't easy, requiring the better part of a full day.

The Hotochrukma were fascinated to watch, with a number of men at first expressing the presumption that Raymondo and Bill would never be able to bring down even so *small* a redwood. As mounds of red chips began to pile up around the cutters' feet at the base of the tree, however, the Indians began to take the endeavor more seriously.

By the time the partners stopped for a noon meal, they'd completed their undercut and had actually begun a backcut. Fearful that a sudden burst of wind might bring the tree crashing earthward, Bill insisted that the Ohlones keep some distance away while Raymondo and he partook of the food Seagull and Calling Owl brought for them— portions of roast antelope and a small basket full of boiled crawdads gathered that very morning from the shallow waters of the creek.

Once the chief's daughters had left, as was deemed proper, Raymondo and Bill, discovering a comfortable spot in the shade of low-growing laurel and alder, took a siesta during the midday heat. The Indians feigned loss of interest, though Beard was certain curiosity would see to it they were close about when time came for the tree to go over— upslope as Bill calculated matters, for he supposed the bole, in falling upon a brushy slope, would be less likely to shatter apart. Preliminary observations suggested that the wood was somewhat brittle. Most of the redwoods which winds had brought down at one time or another were broken as a result of their falls.

After lunch the two axemen began to hew away once more, Bill from one side, Raymondo from the other. Perhaps an hour later, with the two now taking turns at cutting, the moment of victory over the tree was at hand. With the first faintly discernible cracking and straining sounds from within the heartwood, Raymondo put his axe aside and undertook the task of convincing the Hotochrukma to move back, away from the stricken redwood—a precaution against *barberchairing*, should Beard's calculations prove incorrect and the big conifer slip backward off its stump and come crashing down in a direction opposite to what he had planned.

All morning long Pelican Doctor had been conspicuous by his absence, but now, presumably during the last few minutes, he appeared. He stood with his powerful tattooed arms folded over his chest and declined to accept Olivo's judgment that he should move.

Beard put down his axe, walked to where the chief was standing in the fashion of a marble monument, and tried his hand at persuading the older man to move back out of potential harm's way.

Pelican Doctor was resolute.

"Finish killing the tree," he said. "If it is Coyote's will that it falls on top of me, then that is fate. Coyote is more powerful than any other spirit upon the Earth, and he's the one who determines what will come next. Do what you must, Bill Beard."

"If the tree falls and kills you," Bill protested, "then Seagull and Calling Owl will grieve for their father, and they will never be willing to marry the men who caused his death."

"Besides," Raymondo added, "the Hotochrukma would no doubt tie us up and burn us to death."

"That is likely so," Pelican Doctor admitted. "But you cannot leave the tree the way it is. Children might come to play beneath it, and then the wind might blow it over and kill them all. No, you must finish what you have begun."

Raymondo looked at Bill, who shrugged his shoulders. Were his calculations correct? Had he judged the angles properly? The afternoon was very still, and so no chance burst of wind was likely to redirect the tree at the last, most crucial moment. . . . All his skills, all his knowledge of cutting timber was, in fact, no more than a boy's knowledge—a trade unplied these seven years except upon those instances when necessity required the manufacture of a new mast or spar. . . .

"All right, you stubborn, humpbacked grizzly," Beard said to the chief, "I'll see if I can drop the damned thing right on top of you. It'll be just like pounding a peg into the earth."

Pelican Doctor glanced up at the redwood, nodded. Bill was certain the old thief was actually on the verge of smiling.

"Perhaps the chief has powerful redwood medicine," Raymondo said.

Bill and Raymondo walked to the tree, and the man from Vermont instructed his cohort to return to where Pelican Doctor was standing—to study the tree's uppermost branches for the least bit of motion—and then, if the tree started down in Pelican Doctor's direction (him standing like a statue of stubbornness incarnate), to try to get him the hell out of there, by whatever means necessary.

"The tree will fall where you planned, no, *hermano*?"

"Of course," Bill replied.

He strode up to the redwood, lifted his axe, and arced the blade back into the rust-red wood at the core. He supposed no more than a couple dozen strokes would be necessary, but the tree fooled him. As he labored on, he could hear some of the men of the village beginning to talk among themselves. A few were laughing. Then the splintering, crunching sounds grew louder.

"It moves! It moves!" Raymondo shouted.

"Timburrr! Timburrr, Gawddamn it!" Beard shouted and then began to scramble, axe in hand, at a ninety degree angle to the direction of fall.

He turned, watched the redwood's crown tilt slowly,

slowly, and then begin to pick up speed. The big tree was going precisely where he had planned for it to fall. Limbs were breaking loose. Smaller trees were shouldered aside, and the redwood came down with a ground-jarring thud, heaved against the slope, and lay still. Bits and pieces of bark and foliage rained from the green canopy above. The forest was silent for a long moment. Then a bluejay began to squawk its indignation at this sudden change in the configuration of the world.

Bill glanced about. The Hotochrukma were all crouching, shielding their heads. Pelican Doctor maintained the posture he'd assumed before the tree went over. And Raymondo Olivo was doing a jig—whether spontaneous in nature or something he'd learned at San Jose Pueblo, Bill did not think to ask.

At that moment Seagull bolted across the meadow, her long hair trailing behind her and her shapely bare breasts jiggling as she ran. With a last bound, and without speaking, Seagull threw herself into his embrace—nearly jolting him over backward in the process.

Utilizing the whip saw—the *misery whip*, as it was known in Vermont woods—Bill and Raymondo cut the bole into numerous sections and then were obliged to quarter each of these by means of an eight-pound maul and steel wedges. Only then, with an abundance of quarters ready at hand and additional rounds available as they were needed, the men began the fine work of cutting redwood shake—shingles that would bring, or so they hoped, a significant price when hauled in to the settlements. With such a man as Jean Paul Martin as their agent and retailer, was not success almost a certainty?

Slowly the stacks of shake began to accumulate. However much the Hotochrukma may have been impressed by the felling of the redwood, this business of cutting shingles could hardly have appealed less to their imaginations. What Bill and Raymondo were doing, as more than one warrior informed them, was no more than creating "squaw wood"—

kindling, and making it out of the worst sort of wood for such a purpose. As any fool knew, fir or even oak burned better.

Pelican Doctor alone seemed concerned with the activities now, and on each of three days he came to observe, said very little, and then turned and walked away. Furthermore, in the lodge in the evening he said virtually nothing—until Raymondo and Bill and Seagull and Calling Owl as well grew concerned that the chief might be thinking about marrying his daughters to one or another of the older men within the tribe or possibly to someone in Kino-te village, off to the north of Hotochruk, across the Santa Cruz Mountains and close by the Bahía del San Francisco.

Then one late afternoon, still about an hour or more before sundown, Pelican Doctor made indication that he wished both his daughters and his two house guests to follow him. The family group walked down the canyon and through the long meadows and the salt marsh to the place where the big creek, its flow greatly diminished by early autumn, wound its way across the beach and then, rebuffed by heaps of sand thrown up by incoming waves, the slack current pooled back on itself and yet did not quite make it all the way to the ocean. As the chief and his daughters and his prospective son-in-laws reached this spot, the red globe out over the ocean began to pulse an almost unreal intensity of violet-crimson, and the effect of this display reflected in the dammed waters of the stream, giving a distinct appearance of blood.

Pelican Doctor motioned to his daughters, and the two girls set off in search of bits and pieces of driftwood that would do to make a fire.

Cormorants, gulls, scoters drifted with the offshore wind, dipping their wings and gliding in above the humans. A few hundred yards down the beach, a number of seals and sea lions cavorted grotesquely about on the sand, one large bull in the group occasionally belching with great gusto and bellowing in a manner that was neither a roar nor a moan. In the aftermath of such a display of sound, the dominant animal would turn his head, square his shoulders in the direction of the human intruders upon his domain, and glare accusingly.

Pelican Doctor scooped out a hollow in damp sand near the wave-created dam across the creek, and here he assembled the wood his daughters brought. He indicated that he'd be pleased if Bill were to save them all some time by utilizing his mechanical flint and steel fire-striker to light the bonfire.

Not until flames had begun to dance in the wind did Pelican Doctor stand up.

"What's wrong, Father?" Seagull asked.

"Have we done something to displease you?" Calling Owl continued. "You must tell us what we've done wrong so that we won't repeat the offense. None of us wishes to displease you."

At that moment they heard a strange noise—whether caused by a current of wind whipping through a grove of scrub pine back away from the beach or by a coyote whose cry was distorted by distance and the sounds of incoming waves. But at that signal instant Pelican Doctor began to speak, his first uttered syllables causing Bill to startle and catch his breath.

"Yesterday afternoon," the chief said, "I walked far up into the mountains until I reached those high meadows where wind blows constantly. Off to the west, out across the restless ocean, the sun was passing into the dark world, where an opening is said to exist between the fourth and fifth waves. Clouds along the horizon came suddenly into color, glowing red and yellow, like fire itself—so that I almost believed I could hear a hissing of flame and water. Instead I was allowed to see something—a series of images that floated in the air, above me and below me, ghostly forests—except that the trees had all vanished. I tell you, I could see nothing for a great distance around me except stumps that were cut very much like the one you, Raymondo, and you, William, created when you cut down the tree in order to impress the people with your skill.

"At this point," the chief continued, "the face of Coyote

came to me. He wasn't like one of the little song dogs, you understand, but rather like a great man who wore a hat of woven tules and such a coat as is worn by an officer of the Leather Jackets. Eagle and Hummingbird sat on each of his shoulders, but they said nothing at all.

"He laughed and asked me if I liked his new clothing. I couldn't answer, but Coyote Man continued by saying he'd taken the garment from a dead Whiteman, one who'd been crushed by a falling tree. Then he laughed. He tilted back his head and howled for a time, so that Eagle was obliged to flap his wings in order to retain his balance, and Hummingbird leaped up and stood upon the air. When Coyote was finished, he pointed to the many stumps that were still visible in the glowing colors of the sunset, and he said that this was how all the forests would look eventually. Yes, and when the trees were cut down to make boards and shingles, then the spirits of the dead would have nowhere to stay. They would all be hurled into the sky, and when they returned to the ground, there would be so many people that soon nothing would remain for anyone to eat. After that, Coyote Man told me, nearly everyone would die."

"Even the Hotochrukma?" Seagull asked, her eyes wide and gleaming in the firelight now that darkness had begun to set in.

"Coyote didn't mean that our people alone had died," the chief explained. "No, even though the Hotochrukma and the other Ohlones vanished first, what happened was far worse than that. Later the Mexican Spanish and White-face people from far away became very numerous, and then they too all lay down and died. Many of the animal people died also, the grizzly bear and the mountain lion and the condor who rules the air. Everywhere I looked there was death. Coyote didn't explain all this, but I understood.

"I saw one man cut off his sister's leg and begin to eat her flesh—even though she was still alive and screamed terribly. There were many other frightening things also, and I wished to close my eyes, to turn away just as though I were still a small child. . . .

"In the end, there was only darkness, and nothing had any form to it. Nothing except Coyote Man, and he became greater and greater until he filled all of space and all of time. Yes, Coyote and his laughter, which caused the mountains themselves to shudder, just as when the ground sometimes trembles beneath our feet and causes the great trees to sway for a short time."

Pelican Doctor was silent for several moments, and then he coughed and cleared his throat.

"The chief has had a very powerful dream," Raymondo said, his voice hushed. "I can only guess at its meaning. Perhaps Bill Beard and I should not cut the redwood trees? Perhaps we should go elsewhere?"

Pelican Doctor shook his head.

"No," he replied as he steadied his breathing in the aftermath of remembering his great dream. "Coyote has shown me what truly will happen, that is what I believe. No one can change the future of things, for when the Great Dreamer tires of one world, he wipes it all out and creates another, *P'an' tanzhi*. Coyote has had to build many different worlds for the Dreamer of Things, and he will have to build many more. We who are human do not control these matters. We are witnesses only, and we must not cry out or bemoan what is going to happen to us and to everything that is around us. Instead we must be true to ourselves. We must live with honor. We must fight for those things which are precious to us, even though death eventually defeats all. Then we become one with the trees, or perhaps we pass into what my grandfather called World Beyond This One, I don't know."

"Father . . ." Seagull cried out, "you must explain what you mean. I am your daughter, but I still don't understand. . . ."

The fire had burned back down, and only a few flames danced above a mound of glowing orange-red coals. Pelican Doctor knelt and placed additional sticks of wood upon the diminished blaze. Next, from the sealskin purse he wore about his middle, he withdrew that full "scalp"—that is, the hair and the entire skin of the face cured into leather, with strangely elongate holes for eyes, nostrils, and mouth, the latter framed by a short and carefully cut beard which resembled, in Bill's imagination, a small scrub brush. Uttering some words the American didn't understand, Pelican Doctor placed the "scalp" over the renewed flames. The burning hair gave off a decidedly unpleasant odor.

"I love my daughters very much," the chief said, almost as though thinking out loud. "I know what is in their hearts. Seagull and Calling Owl wish to scratch the faces of Señor Beard and Señor Olivo—and so that is how it will be. . . ."

The chief stood up.

"I have thought it through," he said. "You mustn't harm the greatest of the trees, for those have always been like gods to my people. They are giants who speak to us in many ways. But the lesser trees you may cut. I think you'll need to find other men to work for you—not my people, but those who know how to use the tools of metal. I think you will work hard and will succeed—I heard that in Coyote's laughter also. Bring me the bride price that I requested, and we'll celebrate these marriages by means of a great feast. Perhaps the time of darkness and death that Coyote showed me in my vision is still many years from now. How could mere humans, even if their numbers were like those of the grasshoppers in late summer, how could we manage to cut down so many trees? Yet that's what I saw in my vision. For now, then, we'll live our lives in the present, and when the proper time comes for us to die, we must die well."

Raymondo and Bill sold their first load of shingles in Santa Cruz. They received a good price and thereupon retired to Villa de Branciforte, where the one-eyed Spaniard was able to procure a few more firearms—half a dozen pistols (in something less than perfect condition) and a quantity of gunpowder and lead. Thereafter Raymondo and Bill retired to the local *symposium*, where they had a drink or two. While they were there, however, they received a bit of intelligence that inspired them to toss off their last drinks, pay the tab, and beat a hasty retreat back into the mountains.

None other than Fray Orontes, the *mesonero* insisted, would be visiting at the Mission Santa Cruz for the next month or so—overseeing the formal catechisms of the mysteries of Christ to two dozen or so Ohlone recruits, children and young people brought in from Huris-tak village on the Pajaro River. Furthermore, the Santa Cruz detachment of Leather Jackets had been reinforced—perhaps by as many as two hundred men, some soldiers having been dispatched northward from Monterey, while others had accompanied Orontes on the road across the mountains from San José. Speculation ran rampant among the patrons of the *taberna*. Was a Peruvian attack imminent? Russian? A pirate siege?

Were the soldiers loyal to Spain, or had they sided with the revolutionaries?

9

Leather Jackets

The Russians," Olivo said, "perhaps they will attack. Who am I to speak of politics? No, I am just an Indio, and so the governor never consults with me. But I think Arguello, when he was in control, he should never have traded with these Russians. He should have attacked them and driven them away from the place they call Fort Ross. Two years ago when Sola first took power, he interrupted trade with the Russians. Señor Castro and a Russian called Boris Tarakanof were arrested and sent to Mexico on the very same ship that Sola had come north on. The priests at San Jose, they were all speaking of this matter, even as they were counting their silly beads. To trade with Americans, though, that makes sense—for such an arrangement has provided many goods that we would otherwise never have gotten, and besides, I have gained a *Sancho de Beard*."

Raymondo, Bill was firmly convinced, would himself have made an admirable governor. He was a man blessed with extremely keen hindsight.

There was yet another possibility, of course, one that had nothing whatsoever to do with hostilities between Mexico and Mother Spain—but did concern Pelican Doctor and his people. Was it conceivable that Governor Sola could be so concerned about one "rebellious" Indian village that he would order full military action against it?

Olivo and Beard deviated from their previous practice. Orontes or no Orontes, they deemed it necessary that they pass by the military encampment which they had learned was just north of the village. A number of Leather Jackets had indeed made bivouac on the beach close by the headlands, but the atmosphere, so far as one could judge, was hardly appropriate to a state of military alert.

The partners drove their ox-drawn rig along the coast road on their return to Hotochruk, but they perceived no other signs of military preparation such as might have been evident if the Leather Jackets were indeed planning to move against Pelican Doctor.

"Nevertheless," Raymondo argued, shifting in the buckboard's seat to take a glance at the horses who trailed along behind, their hooves making regular *clop-clopping* sounds on the packed clay of the roadway, "there is certainly some reason why additional soldiers have been sent to Santa Cruz. If this many Leather Jackets attack Pelican Doctor's village, how will the Hotochrukma defend themselves? Not even with the few guns we bring will the men be able to protect their women and their children. We must warn Pelican Doctor—we must convince him to move his people farther back into the mountains, where they will be safe."

"Perhaps some of the other villages have attempted to fight back," Bill replied, "Sokel or Aulin-tak. . . ."

"No one in Villa de Branciforte said such a thing. It may be that the Mexican authorities have learned the Spanish intend to send a man o' war to bombard the town. However, that really doesn't make sense either. . . ."

Beard ran his fingers through his long hair and then adjusted the inch-wide leather band about his forehead.

"The Spanish cannot hope to defeat the Mexican rebels by attacking Santa Cruz. Santa Cruz is nothing. Why not Monterey or Yerba Buena? More to the point, why should they concern themselves with California at all? This land of ours is far away from anything that genuinely concerns Mexico."

"We don't even know whether these Leather Jackets

are loyal to Spain or to Mexico," Raymondo pointed out.
"Yet perhaps it is all one and the same. Maybe the new
troops simply intend to round up all those outlaws who stay
close by Branciforte. The government wishes to make this
area safe for further settlers. . . ."

"If so," Bill laughed, "then we should offer to let the
men of Branciforte come help us with the cutting of trees
into shingles. We must save their hides and also put them
to use. . . ."

Beard and Olivo passed by the amphitheaterlike cove
where the girls had caught the two of them with their pants
down, so to speak, and they continued along the grassy
bluffs overlooking the Pacific Ocean, vast and blue and
gleaming with sunlight, a sea whose extent reached half
around the world. Waves hurled themselves in against
jagged rock formations, and white-winged gulls drifted on
the air, sometimes rising for no apparent reason and then
falling once again, then winging past in apparent curiosity
or the hope that the humans might have about their persons
(and therefore would obviously be interested in sharing)
some scraps of bread.

At Hotochruk Creek the two turned inland, traversing
the meadows and finally riding back into the dense seclusion of the canyon itself—to the place where the great
double redwood grew among a gathering of its lesser
relatives, and the lodges of Pelican Doctor's people stood
close by the streamside.

A group of boys caught sight of Beard and Olivo, the
lads stationed at the foot of the canyon as scouts. Two of
them ran off immediately, while the others came forward,
wishing to inspect whatever cargo the wagon might carry.

A quarter of a mile farther along, Seagull and Calling
Owl appeared. Having been told by the boys that their
friends were on the way in, the young ladies stationed
themselves demurely beside the trail and waited. Bill
and Raymondo dismounted from the ox cart immediately,
and each embraced his respective sweetheart. Seagull and
Beard even indulged in a kiss—since no other members of
the village were about. Ohlone protocol certainly didn't

prohibit a show of affection between unmarried men and women, though excessive public display was considered improper. Such activities were carried on, by general consent, in *secret places* which were in fact known to everyone—away from the lodges themselves—thickets of alder or willow or perhaps beneath the spreading branches of a nutmeg tree.

Seagull's bare breasts were too much temptation, and Bill leaned his head to one side, kissed, and then bit softly at a nipple.

"I have heard of men like you." Seagull laughed. "When our little ones come, they'll have to fight you if they wish to nurse. Stop, now. Raymondo and Calling Owl will see what you're doing, Bill Beard. . . ."

When the foursome at length reached the village, Pelican Doctor accepted the weapons the partners had acquired and indicated his pleasure that his prospective sons-in-laws were making such fine progress in fulfilling the bride prices he'd demanded for his two beautiful daughters.

In anticipation of yet a further payment in the near future, the chief encouraged Bill and Raymondo again to load the cart with shingles (these having already been manufactured) and to return forthwith to their friends in Santa Cruz and Monterey.

"We've learned something," Olivo said, "that may be important for the safety of this village. It's said that two hundred additional Leather Jackets have been sent to Santa Cruz."

"Are you certain of this?"

Bill Beard nodded agreement with what Raymondo had just spoken.

"We didn't see the troops, Pelican Doctor, but everyone in Branciforte was aware of their presence. At the pueblo there's even some talk of an invasion by Peruvians—or a bombardment. I believe it's certain that something's about to happen. What that something is, unfortunately, we don't know."

"At other times," Raymondo remarked, "the Leather Jackets have been used to pacify Indians, as you're aware.

I was but a child when I was taken from my own mother and
father in that fashion. The same thing happened to you,
Pelican Doctor. The priests, they wish to feed all of us to
their Jesus god, and they use the soldiers to achieve their
purposes."

"Christ is their Kind One," Pelican Doctor said. "We
do not need to fear him. It's unfortunate that the Mexican
Spanish fail to listen to their god. I think maybe the Spanish
were the ones who killed that Jesus, long ago, so that they
themselves could then do whatever they wished."

A debate on the nature of theology, Beard realized,
had precious little to do with any immediate threat to
Hotochruk, whether that threat was real or imagined.

"Raymondo believes the chief should move his village
to some place back into the mountains," Bill said, "some
spot that is safer. . . ."

Pelican Doctor studied the two men.

"Maybe we're not so powerless as you think, Bill
Beard. In any case, it's better to wait until we see whether
there's actually any danger at all. Possibly the Leather
Jackets are to be sent somewhere else in one of the big
Spanish canoes. We will not begin to fight until we're
required to do so."

Wishing to take no unnecessary risks, Raymondo and Bill
conveyed their next load of shingles all the way south to
Monterey, even at the expense of two or three days of extra
travel. The partners were, after all, under some obligation
to Jean Paul Martin—even though the market was less
convenient.

As matters turned out, their merchant friend made the
journey well worth their time, for he was extremely pleased
to see Señors Beard and Hermes and thereupon purchased
the entire load without so much as a bit of friendly bickering
over price. The three men drank wine and concluded that
they indeed had much in common.

Jean Paul listened to Bill's talk of the timber industry in
the Maine woods—and of the log drives down the rivers to

such places as Bangor, where mills with water-driven or steam-driven saws sliced the logs into boards. The forests of California, Martin insisted, were certainly much more extensive than those of New England, and the trees were both much larger and much taller. In all the world, he asserted, there were no trees so great as some of the redwoods.

Bill agreed readily enough, and Raymondo smiled in such a way that his friend presumed he was recalling a certain discussion the two conducted that time while on horseback and muleback in the mountains to the east of San José.

"Yet here," Bill complained, "we have no big rivers. The Pajaro, for instance, is hardly a river at all."

"But the Nem Seyoo, it is a great river," Olivo protested. "It flows into Bahía del San Francisco and comes out of the long valley to the east. An old Wintun man who visited San José Pueblo claimed that Nem Seyoo begins far to the north, in a desert that lies beyond a spirit mountain that is forever covered with snow. If that's true, then somewhere along such a river there must be trees. Besides, could the cargo ships not simply sail up Nem Seyoo to where the trees grow?"

"Good point, good point," Beard admitted. "Gents, it's clear that we have to look at the overall picture. I tell you, this California is a land of immense opportunity. Hell, whole logs can be cut up into sections and tied together to form big rafts of timber. These can be towed by ships. But California will have to have far more people than it does now, many more. What good's lumber if no one wishes to build anything with it? We must have a proper market, even if that market's far away. Well, well. In the final analysis, trees grow in many places, but only here does one find redwoods."

Jean Paul Martin shook his head.

"*Eh bien.* Such trees are also said to exist in the mountains to the south of Monterey, among the Santa Lucias and the Ventanas. But to the north of Bahía del San Francisco, that is where the true giants are rumored to grow. Three years ago I met a pair of British trappers—men of the Hudson's Bay Company. They said they'd traveled through hundreds of miles of redwoods, some of the trees so huge it was not possible for me to believe what they said, *en vérité*. Ah, gentlemen, perhaps the future we dream of is not so far away as we suppose. Who can foretell the future?"

"In fact," Olivo laughed, "I have a better idea. . . ."

"Raymondo's always got a better idea," Bill said.

"Do not listen to this Señor Beard. He will tell you Bill is short for Benjamin—something of that sort. He is the kind of man who would complain even if he were hung with a new rope. You want the truth, *verdad*? Very well, then, here is the truth. The only hope for mankind is complete annihilation. Even the good Saint Paul believed something highly analogous to what I have just said. He was a very grouchy saint, that one."

"Indians and Irishmen," Beard shrugged, "have never been able to hold their . . . *cerveza*."

"A pox on the Spanish and the Mexicans as well," Jean Paul Martin said. "Friends of me, I think it is time for California to be a nation of its own. Is a big land, a good land. One day it will be a very rich land, *à Dieu!* And now that most of the sea otters and fur seals are gone, we must look to different kinds of exports—redwood lumber, for instance."

Hence, with the prospect of profits as both the simple incentive and the glue to bind the relationship, Martin secured for Beard and Olivo a second wagon, this one drawn by a pair of well-heeled mules.

As quickly as possible, Martin indicated, they were to bring in two full loads of shingles. Jean Paul claimed to have numerous buyers near San Diego. More importantly, he had the ability to make necessary arrangements. An American frigate bound for New Orleans would be sailing southward in a month, and with luck this new cargo would be aboard.

Even sales abroad, Martin suggested, were within the realm of the possible—and not just for shingles. Redwood beams and planks as well would find a ready market. Practicality, however, insisted that such cargo should be loaded either at Santa Cruz or at some other place nearer to the cutting area.

Beard agreed, suggesting a landing site some twelve or fifteen miles to the north of Santa Cruz—a spot he was able to locate on Martin's charts of the coast. To this place, Martin said, he would dispatch a sailing craft capable of taking aboard the desired quantity of shingles. For Raymondo and Bill, it was simply a matter of getting the damned things cut.

The possibilities, of course, were immense—just as Bill had foreseen all along. What was needed was a full-scale logging operation, complete with a gang of New England timber fallers, a bunch of rowdies from Bangor. For the real question was this: could two men manage to meet the demand for the product? Quite evidently, Bill and Raymondo, working without assistance, could not. Without a genuine woods gang, the partners could do no more than to eke out a common living. But with a gang of working men—yes, with such a crew, a company was possible.

Hermes and Beard, Shinglers Extraordinaire.

Martin was able to secure for them the tools that would be necessary to outfit the *timber beasts*, as well as four old Spanish-issue muskets and a keg of powder, the latter hidden well down under the rest of the cargo.

In addition, Jean Paul convinced the partners to do one thing further—and that was to write out a formal letter to Governor Sola, a letter which Martin himself would endorse. In this appeal they gave a general explanation of the business venture they proposed. The thrust of the letter was that they were requesting that a land grant be awarded to the two of them, jointly. The land they had in mind? Some extensive groves of redwoods to the north of Santa Cruz—not agricultural land, but mere forest—mere trees which they proposed as natural resource to be developed for the general good of Alta California, with lumber to be utilized both within the boundaries (indefinite) of the province and with excess to be shipped to Mexico or to whatever foreign ports might provide a ready market.

Beard made a rough copy of one of Jean Paul Martin's maps, indicating the mountainous region to the north of Santa Cruz Mission and Villa de Branciforte—an area five miles by ten miles, some thirty-two thousand acres in all, through which, as he and Raymondo had discovered, ran the upper San Lorenzo River. Official maps didn't indicate either the river's source or much of anything else away from the settled areas.

Olivo shook his head.

"I guess we might as well think big," he said. "Otherwise, Governor Sola will suppose we are *insano*, *loco*, *y frenetico*."

"*Eh bien*, Monsieur Hermes, it is also well to use your actual name as we write out this document. We must be legal. In case you succeed, no doubt you will wish to be able to take title to your land. Olivo and Barrington—that was quite a stunt they pulled, *très dangereaux*, kidnapping the *prêtre*, *non?* One is Indio, one is *Americaine*. Do I guess correctly? You, Raymondo, are Olivo—and you, sir, Barrington, *n'est ce-pas?*"

Bill glanced at Ray, turned back to Martin. If the Frenchman knew all along and hadn't turned them in, then apparently he was more interested in doing business than in apprehending fugitives.

"William Beard of Vermont." The American grinned, once again offering his hand. "And this is my partner, Raymondo Olivo."

Jean Paul Martin laughed.

"So—I was at least partially correct. Alta California is a large place, but it also a very small one."

During the ride north, the partners concluded that even the risk of a run-in with the wretched Father Orontes was worth it, for they desperately required the services of a dozen men. They'd attempt to do their hiring from among the drifters and deserters and criminals of various sorts who lived close about the highly irregular Villa de Branciforte.

Indeed, the boot of authority had been placed on the neck of Branciforte—by which figure of speech one means merely to note that the *alcalde* of Santa Cruz, backed by a small detachment of *caballeria* under the command of one Patrón Lopez Diego, had entered Branciforte village and had presented warrants sufficient for the arrests of some eleven men, five of whom were actually discovered to be within the village, while the remainder were either not present in the first place or had managed to make their escape before the Leather Jackets could identify them. The pall of this act of civil government hung heavily over the village, and numerous men not specified in the indictments were in fact making preparations for immediate departure.

When Olivo and Beard announced they were willing to pay monthly wages to a dozen men fit and able to handle both axe and whipsaw—the work to be performed in the mountains some fifteen miles distant from Branciforte and Santa Cruz—they had more takers than they had jobs. Transportation then became the crucial issue, and so, given the circumstances, they were able to hire only such able-bodied workers as had their own horses or mules.

As the laws of fate and chance would have things, among the men hired was the American who, several years earlier, had instructed Raymondo Olivo in the art and craft of shoeing horses—one Samson Flowers, an American like Beard, and like Beard, a man who'd also jumped ship—in Monterey, actually, the previous September. Flowers, however, was not a New Englander. Raised in the village of St. Louis, he'd made his way upriver for the purposes of trapping. He claimed to have known Charbonneau—to have been in the same Hidatsa village with the old fox of the mountains and his wife Sacajawea when those two left to become part of the Lewis and Clark expedition.

Flowers subsequently, or so he claimed, made his way across the continent on his own and eventually became a trapper for the Hudson's Bay Company, had made three ventures south to California, and had ended up on a British trading vessel intent upon buying otter pelts and fur seal. The schooner set anchor in Monterey, and the unpredictable Samson Flowers simply went ashore and stayed there.

Tall and muscular and only in his late twenties, veteran frontiersman though he was, he wore buckskins and a brace of long knives and carried a short-barreled Hawken flintlock—quite an impressive individual, almost like a character out of some tall tale.

With the "logging crew" selected and one wagon with foodstuffs and incidentals, they set out for the redwood groves—not those close about Hotochruk, but a few miles to the south, near the headwaters of the San Lorenzo—the site of the proposed land grant. Rather than take any further risks with either Church or state, Bill and Raymondo and a dozen new varlets made their way northward, the odd little caravan working toward the back of the Santa Cruz Mountains. They proceeded to the upper basin of the San Lorenzo. From there they'd be required to construct some sort of wagon trail to the coast, to one or another of several coves, where with luck Martin's schooner could make a landing and take on a cargo of shingles. Winch lines from headland to beach below would be sufficient to belay the cargo down, bundles of shake secured with hempen twine.

OLIVO & BEARD

It wasn't much, not yet, but Raymondo and Bill both considered their enterprise as founded and fairly begun. They had, after all, pledged contracts, a perfectly salable product, and a crew who were certainly able-bodied enough if only they could be persuaded to work.

Camp was set up at the proposed mill site, not far from a grove of immense redwoods, several of which had limbs thicker than the usual run of merchantable pines or spruces in New England. These giants, however, weren't the objects of Olivo and Beard's commercial affections. Not only were such trees deemed holy to the Hotochrukma and hence certain to bring on bad medicine if cut, but also they were just too damned big to handle, even if the partners desired to do so.

Much more to the point: here grew extensive groves of relative "toothpicks," both redwood and a variety of fir or spruce, many of which were virtually as tall and with as great diameters as the giant redwoods themselves.

Perhaps it was something about the soil of California, Bill reflected, or some chemical thing having to do with the proximity of the Pacific Ocean, that caused trees to grow to far greater age and hence to far greater size. In any case, for the next several days the men were engaged in felling small firs no more than two feet at the butt—trees that nonetheless reached a hundred fifty feet or so in height. These would be the timbers needed for the construction of the mill.

Several redwoods were felled also, trees somewhat larger than the firs. Half the crew would engage in the manufacture of shingles while the remaining men were putting up the frame of the mill, a structure to be located downstream from a series of cascades on the San Lorenzo—against that hoped-for time when, by delivering current through a flume, one would be able to turn a big water wheel and so power the axles and belts that would drive saws.

A week later, with operations moving smoothly and with a steady clatter coming from the four shingle jigs, Raymondo and Bill concluded that they'd take the opportunity to return to Hotochruk village. Both men were yearning to be with their women once more, and, of course, they had weapons to deliver to Pelican Doctor—yet another installment on the bride prices to which they'd agreed.

Under the circumstances, it was necessary to designate someone officially in charge during their absence. Bill suggested Samson Flowers.

Raymondo looked doubtful but was willing to go along with the choice—for the moment, at least.

10

Consummation by the Sea

The boys whose task it was to act as scouts obviously detected their presence as Bill and Raymondo crossed the meadows before the creek forks, for the partners in crime and business soon heard yips of coyotes and the cries of screech owls as well, both things highly unusual before sundown. Always on previous occasions when the partners had been gone for a few days, Seagull and Calling Owl would await them along the narrow portion of the trail, below the village itself. This time, however, the ladies weren't there.

As Bill and Raymondo entered the village, they realized preparations were under way for a time of festivities. The unmarried women and young wives and boys had brought in a bumper harvest of acorns, and older women supervised the process of leaching out the *suk*, the bitterness, and then the grinding of the kernels into meal which was ultimately to be stored as a kind of coarse flour for use throughout the winter—meal that could be mixed with water and hence turned into a variety of bread and cakelike substances. Golden-brown globes of the buckeye were also milled, and here the leaching took longer and was more involved. Untreated, the buckeye was quite toxic. Indeed, raw buckeye was sometimes smashed to a paste and then put into a creek to poison fish.

The matrons now insisted that Beard and Olivo listen to a full accounting of the gathering and milling of the sacred acorn, and all the while they kept pulling at the fringes of the men's jackets and quarreling good-naturedly with one another and grinning in a most foolish manner.

Bill and Raymondo were obliged to eat a few freshly-cooked balls of acorn bread with blackberries and gooseberries in them—the latter, fortunately, having had their spines removed before being baked in acorn dough. The result, actually, was quite tasty.

But clearly something unusual was afoot—possibly some sort of general mischief, as the partners supposed. Perhaps it was no more than a coincidence that tonight would mark the full moon—full moon and an equinox at the same time. All the prerequisites for human lunacy were in place.

Eventually Pelican Doctor came to rescue them from the Witches of the Acorn Coven, and the partners accompanied the chief to his lodge—where, as they devoutly hoped, Seagull and Calling Owl would be waiting. Such, however, was not the case. The chief had a fire burning in the pit outside his lodge, and he motioned for Beard and Olivo to sit down. Almost as though he were one of the women, Pelican Doctor began to talk of virtually nothing. An autumn salmon run had likewise been plentiful, as Bill and Raymondo already knew, though one doubted that any great number of fish ever bothered to come up this stream the Ohlones designated simply as Big Creek. Fish that did commit to the stream, however, could go no farther than the broad pool at the bottom of Stone Face Falls. Indeed, riffles below this pool were regarded as the best of all fishing locations along the creek.

Pelican Doctor explained that a final phase of the season of food gathering would result in a mass assembly upon the beach where the creek ran to the Pacific—for purposes of digging clams and harvesting mussels and abalones. This picnic on the shore was to occur the following day. Equinox time had come, and offerings were to be made to a god known as Grandfather Sun, husband to Grandmother Earth.

For a moment the worship of the sun struck Beard as odd, almost out of place. Most god-beings in the Ohlone pantheon were animal spirits—Coyote, Eagle, Hummingbird, Grizzly, Mountain Lion, Deer, or Condor. Other entities included the Grand Dreamer, World Maker (when such tasks were not being handled by Coyote), the Star People, Earth, Moon, and now the Sun. When one got right down to it, however, what could be more obvious? Without warmth and light there could be no life at all.

Bill toyed with the notion that all religion whatsoever might have begun with prayers of thanks, these directed at the sun, but he gave up on the idea when the specter of the Wrathful Father and Satanic Lucifer began to rise up, these titanic forces inculcated in his awareness when he was but a boy back in New England, unable to defend himself against the adult's supposed capacity for logic—against the all but inhuman doctrines of the Presbytery, the Church authorities and their perpetual fears of hellfire and damnation.

Beard granted, however, that as a means of inflicting a conscience upon the otherwise savage condition known as childhood, he really had no quarrel with the practice—and none, he supposed, could do it better than the New Englanders.

Render unto me the little children. . . .

Pelican Doctor asked if Raymondo and Bill had brought him any presents. Always, he assured them, he enjoyed receiving presents. Indeed, as it turned out, he was very pleased with the weapons they took out of their saddlebags. Though they were still very far from the chief's apparent goal of arming every adult male in the village, yet their persistence showed good intentions.

"Calling Owl and Seagull," Raymondo asked as soon as opportunity presented itself, "they are all right? They're not ill? It's very strange that they didn't come out to meet us. . . ."

Pelican Doctor nodded.

"You, Bill and Raymondo, you cut down the trees, and yet you don't touch the giant redwoods which contain the protecting spirits of our ancient dead?"

The partners assured the chief that they had fallen no redwoods of the magnitude he suggested.

"It is good. I am glad to hear that. Now it's time for Raymondo and Bill to marry the women they have chosen. I know what is in your hearts, my sons, and so I know that you'll bring me more weapons as soon as you're able to get them. No other men in Hotochruk could ever have paid such a price for their women. Nor would I have asked so much of you two had not the safety of my people depended upon it."

"We understand, Pelican Doctor," Bill responded. "Have Seagull and Calling Owl been sent away from the village for some reason?"

"No," he replied. "They are here. They're not far away. A man who is about to be married must not see the woman he marries until he meets her in a *runaway hut*, a small *iwano*. Now I will tell you about marriage among my people. Perhaps I'll tell you some things that you do not know. Among all the Ohlones it is this way—and that's one reason why the Catholic priests want to change us. But why should we change? Our way has worked for us since the time of First Man and First Woman. As with all creatures, male and female do not always get along, even though they must come together in order to bring new little ones into the world.

"For this reason my people have not bound the woman to the man with iron chains, such as the Mexican Spanish use with their wagons and other machinery or to control the grizzlies they capture for the purpose of putting them in pits with bulls. No, we allow only the *chaka*, string made from the milkweed pods. We believe a woman should stay with her mate only as long as she wishes to do that. A bride price is asked, an amount of shell money appropriate to the woman's standing within her village. But the father who takes this money must be prepared to return it if one day his daughter decides she does not wish to remain with her husband.

"Spanish Catholics call such a thing *divorce*, and they say it is from the Devil, one who is very much like Coyote. But we feel it's better for the woman to find another husband if she can than to remain with one who does not please her or who abuses her. Coyote approves of women who change their minds, provided only that there are good reasons. When a woman divorces her husband, she takes her children with her, and the father may not steal them back again.

"Among the Catholics, a man may have only one wife, but he may have more than one mistress. I learned much, you see, while I was their captive. But in truth, I do not understand this distinction. With us it is presumed a man will have just one wife. If he is a chief, if he gains wealth, then he is permitted to have more, if he wishes to do so—but I don't think that's a good idea, either."

Beard and Olivo agreed—at the same time wondering when the chief's lecture on matrimony among the Hotochrukma would end and where Seagull and Calling Owl were hiding.

"You, Raymondo, come from Saklan, in the north. I am told that a man of those people may marry not only one woman, but also his wife's sister or even her daughter or some other relative. Perhaps in Saklan there are not enough men to go around, I don't know."

"Yes," Raymondo replied, "I believe that's true—about marrying sisters or cousins—but I wouldn't be willing to do such a thing. I was only a boy when I lived in Saklan—and after that the priests attempted to turn me into a Catholic. I resisted; but nonetheless, probably I came to believe as the Holy Word prescribes. I wish to have no other woman than Calling Owl. I will be faithful to her. . . ."

"We will smoke tobacco now," Pelican Doctor said. "Tomorrow evening after we have danced on the beach and feasted, my four best warriors will escort each of you in turn to a separate *runaway iwano* made of fresh willow boughs and tule thatch. There you'll find food and drink. After a time, your women will come to you."

Pelican Doctor rose, entered his lodge, and reemerged with his stone medicine pipe. He proceeded to fill the bowl with crumbled leaves of the native tobacco. With a burning twig he lit the pipe and then gestured to the four sacred directions and to the earth and to the sky.

The three men passed the pipe, one to the other, each savoring the taste of smoke.

The Hotochrukma children and old women had spent the afternoon up and down the length of the beach and beyond the headlands to either side, collecting mounds of driftwood and dried tules and broken-off segments of pine and fir boughs from along the margins of the creek, all these piled into a great heap some eight or ten feet high, and to this accumulation of burnable material would be added the element of sacred fire.

Sundown brooded over the vast Pacific—the horizon glowing crimson and silver to gold, light suffusing long streamers of fog out across the restlessly heaving waters: and at the moment when the scarlet globe of the sun itself disappeared behind a lip of fog, leaving behind a crust of silver-orange metal, as if a ship's smithy had drawn a steel strap directly from the furnace and then plunged its radiant life into a trough full of cold saltwater, Pelican Doctor, chief of the Hotochruk Ohlone band, struck fire to a wadding of tule fibers and placed this clot at the foot of the stack.

Flames emerged, and then, within a matter of moments, the whole mound blazed up, sending showers of sparks into gathering darkness of shadowed, salt-smelling air as waves surged in against jagged dark outlines of sandstone, hitting, hissing, spitting, and then sucking back once again. Pelican Doctor opened a small container of pollen that had been gathered months earlier. This magic powder possessed great medicine, or so the people professed to believe. Then, with a flourish, the chief sprayed the pollen over the leaping flames.

On the high-tide bench above, beyond a cluster of driftwood logs, slung in deerskin pouches and in intricately woven baskets, was an array of foods—a little of virtually everything that Ohlone husbandry produced.

Raymondo and Bill stood in a group then with Pelican Doctor and several of the other men, watching as young people spontaneously entered into a dance about the circle of the big fire, a dance whose various movements and gestures suggested that, in the ancient beginning at least, it had been a dance of seduction and of courtship. As was often the case, the young women of Hotochruk were naked from the waist upward, their arms, breasts, and abdomens glistening with a fragrant oil of some sort. Some of the dancers' faces were marked by chin tattoos, traditionally a zigzag line descending from either side of the mouth, bounding triple straight markings. By firelight the gyrating women seemed strangely nonhuman, ghostlike.

"None of this is happening," Bill said to Raymondo. "You and I, old friend, we're asleep back in our quarters at the pueblo—and tomorrow we'll once again take up the monumental task of cleaning the Augean Stables. Everything we see is but an illusion. Consider how utterly improbable all of it is—you and I among these people, yes, and preparing to become one with them through a ritual of marriage. The starry sky above is also no more than an illusion, a dream, the sort of vision children have, their minds provoking and exciting them by turns. We must wake up, Raymondo. We must awaken before any final curtain comes down. . . ."

"Perhaps Orontes and his accursed stables, perhaps that was the bad dream, *hermano*."

The chief, who had listened carefully, now used his elbow to nudge Raymondo.

"This Beard," Pelican Doctor grunted, "sometimes he makes good sense, and at other times he makes no sense at all."

"We are visionary madmen," Bill continued, taking

Pelican Doctor's comment as encouragement, "enacting out lives that some other, greater madman has scripted for us. And it's all so much like a waking trance. . . . "

"Sancho Bill," Raymondo crooned, "what we see before us is not a dream but a reality. If Don Quixote believes the cardboard visor will withstand the stroke of an infidel's sword, why then so it will. Life itself is the dream, possibly to be recorded by some author a century and a half from now—possibly some poet who writes novels out of desperation. Yes, the dream. If we awaken, why then we awaken into the Big Silence, *El Silencio Grande*. That is what I think. Instead of twisting your wits and your tongue into knots, look instead to see who is dancing about the fire circle. . . . "

Bill Beard looked to where Olivo pointed.

Seagull. Calling Owl.

Although until this moment unseen—unseen for the past two days—the twin sisters who commanded the partners' hearts had entered into the strange, almost grotesque dance that was being enacted about the blazing fire. Seagull and Calling Owl, both acting flirtatious, seductive, beckoning first to one young man and then to another—and yet the males, inexplicably, seemed intent upon turning away from these advances, turning instead to other young women who presumably more thoroughly captivated their fancies.

Seagull and Calling Owl approached one man after another, and yet no one seemed of a mind to engage in the embraces being offered. Faster and faster the dance swirled. The feet of the young men now—beating upon the sand, sometimes in unison, sometimes not. The men twisted about sideways, their arms in gyration. Yet as to the precise significance of these motions, who could say?

Pelican Doctor began to chuckle. He too was caught up in the frenzy of the dancing, even though he was not a part of it. As Bill stared at his prospective father-in-law, the Vermonter could see in his eyes the condition of transport—as though a spell had been cast upon him. Pelican Doctor continued to chuckle. *Chuckle*. . . .

When Bill looked again, the chief's twin daughters had vanished.

Pelican Doctor as well was no longer where he had been but a moment earlier. Instead a circle of Hotochrukma warriors was closing in about Beard and Olivo.

"Raymondo . . ." Bill called out, feeling suddenly quite helpless.

Olivo shrugged.

"What after all is *tragedia* but a song sung in honor of the sacrificial goat, *el cabra*? Think upon it, Friend Beard."

At this moment the Ohlone warriors surrounded Raymondo and began to lead him away. Next they drew Bill with them, but in a direction opposite to the one in which they had taken Raymondo. The warriors didn't speak, but after perhaps a dozen or so steps they stopped long enough to blindfold their ritual captive.

He was inside a small thatched lodge, one that had been just recently constructed—doubtlessly that very day. A container of fish oil into which a wick had been thrust burned feebly. On a circular bark mat in the center of the opening, baskets of meat, shellfish, acorn mush, and even a small pot of wild honey had been placed.

The ocean is very near. It is very near, and it's speaking to me. What is it saying?

To the rear of the oblong area defined by the lodge was a pallet of grasses and tule down covered over by a sewn rabbitskin blanket.

The wedding bed.

After what seemed like an astonishingly long time, an interval that in all likelihood did not exceed ten minutes, Bill heard shuffling footsteps on the sand outside the lodge wherein he sat. Next the elkhide entryway was pushed to one side, and a woman was rudely thrust in—despite apparent protests.

It was Seagull.

"I do not wish to lie down with you," she said, turning her back to him.

"Gull? What's happened? Is this the usual way of Ohlone marriage?"

"I'm here with you, Bill Beard, and since you're a man and stronger than I am, you are able to force me to lie down with you, even though I should hate it. Do as you will, then, since I'm unable to prevent you."

"What are you talking about, woman? If you've got cold feet—I mean, if you've decided you don't wish to marry me, then, well, hellfire. . . ."

Seagull knelt before him, pressed her face up against his groin.

"It is proper for a Hotochruk woman to resist her husband—to scratch his face," she whispered. "It's necessary for the woman to pretend that she doesn't like what her man does to her."

"A pretense merely?" Bill asked, still genuinely confused by Seagull's strange words and even stranger actions.

She laughed—a laughter that was partly a giggle and partly a wail of delight.

"I'll tell you a very great secret, my *husband*—a secret that Coyote taught First Woman. We like to have you men stick your *pauois* into us. We even like to pet them and lick at them and take them into our mouths. And yet we must always pretend to hate that which we love. Coyote is perverse, and so must women be unless they wish to anger the one who created most of the world."

"Would my lady care for some fresh crabmeat?" Bill asked. "Some acorn cake with honey smeared over it? All this talk is beginning to hurt my head. Let's—"

Then they were in one another's embrace, and Seagull was attempting to assist her man in removing his deerhide clothing.

When her hand found what it sought, she broke into that strange chuckling laughter once again. When she stepped away from the second of her two skirts and stood there as naked as upon the proverbial day she was born, Beard put his arms about her and lifted her. Two strides later he deposited her upon the wedding bed and, now fully aroused, lay down beside her.

"First," she gasped, "I must scratch your face, Bill Beard. If I do not do this thing, all the other women in the village will suppose I am shameless."

It was his turn to laugh now.

"Not true? Not true? Gull, you've got no more shame than a doe in heat . . . just about that much, I'd say. Now lie still while I nuzzle your—"

"My husband talks too much," she replied as she raked her fingernails down over his cheekbones. "This will sting a little, maybe."

"Gull . . . my Gawd, girl, but I do love you. All this marriage ceremony . . . why didn't anyone tell me?"

But then she took him in both hands and leaned forward, her lamplit facial features obscured by the flowing strands of her black hair.

Beard groaned in pleasure and was but dimly aware of the sounds of waves spewing over sands, of waves withdrawing and chasing pebbles along with them, of breakers still a quarter of a mile off the coast booming and booming and booming. After a time they slept the sleep of sexual exhaustion, the two of them covered with perspiration and locked in one another's arms. Perhaps an hour before dawn, however, Seagull awakened her husband and urged him to rise—to go with her.

"Go where, my Gull?"

"Lazy man, always sleeping. Just like the Mexican Espansh. You sure you're not one of them? We go down to the water to bathe. . . ."

Hand in hand by the thin light of predawn, they made their way to the surf and then, together and almost as though on key, they plunged in.

The few days that followed were indeed magic—as Seagull and Bill, and sometimes Calling Owl and Raymondo as well, walked along the beaches or took to horseback and ventured into the fastnesses of the canyons where dense stands of great redwoods grew. Sword ferns were in abundance in these enchanted places, spurting from black, humus-rich earth, marking the hillsides below springs, clustering about twisted liveoaks, or emerging from between gnarled redwood roots. The trees themselves, rising from an understory of bay, azalea, currant, maple, elderberry, and sometimes buckeye, alder, or beech, formed a seemingly endless irregular series of huge tapered columns wrapped in rough red-gray bark. Leafy, ivylike vines (already blushing bright red at the end of summer) grew up the sides of the columns until they were lost to sight amidst high, thick foliage.

Early mornings and late afternoons, however, were Beard's favorites among the great trees, for it was then that broad spars and bars of sunlight came angling down from the interlocked mats of branches high above, and he had almost the impression of walking through the Garden of Eden. Yet if the voice of the Lord were also abroad and roaming about in the garden, Bill was not aware of His august presence. Instead the movements of air among these titanic living forms seemed a virtual whisper, a gentle, restrained, and infinitely patient whisper.

"Such trees," Raymondo said as the four of them rode along together, "*cierto* they are far too large for us to think of cutting down, is it not so? And yet truly, if one had the ability, if one had the proper sort of machine, could one not do it?"

"It could be done," Bill said after stopping for a moment or two to study a particularly immense tree. "In order to move the individual logs once the trees were down, we might have to use explosives to split the things in halves—or in quarters. Get them down to something a few oxen in traces could drag along gracefully. Skid roads and lines—yes, and we could get the devils in to wherever the mill's set up."

"I do not understand all this about cutting the trees," Calling Owl said. "You two make shingles, but why is it necessary to cut down anything? Already there are so many pieces of redwood lying about. I think perhaps Eagle or Coyote has left these logs lying on the ground so that you may use them. . . ."

But Beard wasn't really listening to the words. Bouyed by marriage and by a vision of the future as well, a vision that included mills and docks and saws and all the wonderful buildings that would eventually be constructed out of this redwood, he could see Alta California as a nation unto itself, a nation great and strong in the world's community of nations. Loads of Olivo & Beard redwood would be sent forth on the cargo ships, and redwood houses would appear in such far-off places as Boston, London, Paris, Rome. . . .

Bill and Raymondo and their wives and their Ohlone relatives (if only Guillermo and Raymondo were able to control a few variables) were going to become rich, exceedingly rich. Never had he been more certain of anything.

Seagull pointed excitedly but did not speak.

In the clearing before them were three wild animals not commonly seen together—a grizzly, a wolf, and a mountain lion. One might almost have supposed the three had been engaged in some sort of highly significant conversation.

As the four humans watched, the grizzly and the wolf moved away in opposite directions, disappearing into the denseness of forest. But the mountain lion remained— looked in their direction—seemed totally oblivious to their presence.

The big cat screamed—a scream that was neither pain nor outrage nor loneliness, but perhaps all three of these emotions together, yes, and other feelings as well. For a moment longer the cougar glared at the human beings, and then it seemed to dematerialize—to vanish in a glow of sunlight.

"It is strange," Raymondo said, his voice hardly more than a whisper. "Our horses did not startle—were not aware at all."

"Are you sure we saw what we saw?" Bill asked.

11

The Yokuts Orpheus

The fortunes of both nations and individual men, as Beard supposed, were subject to change—to perpetual alternations of the good and the bad. At the moment, however, the luck of Olivo & Beard was riding a fair sea, with all canvas billowed and the wind constant. Pelican Doctor provided the only sour note, the single augury of potential darkness.

"Something is wrong," the chief announced to his sons-in-law. "I do not know what it is, but my dreams have begun to speak to me. Yesterday morning as I walked along the beach, I discovered three male sea lions dead—three of them all together in a group—and yet I couldn't determine what happened to them. There were no wounds—the creatures hadn't been fighting. Not even the vultures or the ravens came down to touch them. Then I rode the horse Raymondo gave me over here, to San Lorenzo River, to see what you two have built. After we ate dinner last night, the coyotes howled for a long while. We all heard them. That is also very unusual."

"Unusual—for coyotes to howl?" Bill asked.

Raymondo Olivo glanced at Bill Beard—whom he expected to dismiss the old chief's premonition without ever having considered it. Beard, Olivo had noted, seemed constitutionally incapable of paying close attention to any of those things that the conscious intellect was not formed to interpret, though in other ways the man from Vermont was the very paradigm of acuity. He was, after all, a man who understood about *gears and wheels*.

"Yes," Pelican Doctor replied. "It is unusual for the song dogs to sing for such a long time. They do that only during their mating season—and sometimes before the earth shakes. Perhaps that is what it means, then. Maybe tomorrow or the next day the ground will heave beneath our feet."

"What do your dreams tell you?" Raymondo asked. "Are you able to speak of these things?"

"I have grown old." Pelican Doctor laughed. "Perhaps I now worry as though I were some toothless widow woman. My sons-in-law have brought me fine weapons, and I have given these to my warriors. Now we're armed much better than we were before. If the Leather Jackets attack Hotochruk, I believe we will be able to protect our women and children."

"That's what you're worried about?" Beard asked. "Truth to tell, I get the idea that the military boys are more concerned about some Peruvian ship coming in to Monterey and blasting away at the buildings than they are about the Ohlones."

"It may be that you're right," Pelican Doctor said. "But I have told you—the soldiers attacked us before, and that's why I asked you to buy weapons for the people. We must be ready in case the Leather Jackets ever again decide to come after us. Raymondo, do you believe Bill's right? Do I worry about something that doesn't exist? Am I like my silly horse—always supposing a puma is near and has come to get me?"

Olivo cut a small wedge of Salinas Valley cheese from the dark yellow wheel on the chuck wagon cutting board, took a bite, closed one eye, and considered the masklike expression on Pelican Doctor's face.

"There are more soldiers in Santa Cruz now than we have seen for the past couple of months," he said. "But there aren't any rumors of an Indian campaign."

Pelican Doctor stared at the cheese, then back at Raymondo.

"In my dream I see fire," he said. "I see flames burning about the bases of the two great redwoods in Hotochruk. I have dreamed this thing three times now. . . ."

William Beard's world was indeed enchanted—the old vision of his boyhood had come wonderfully, inexplicably, astonishingly true. *The vision of the dark-eyed girl in the forest*. . . . Just as these past few months had put the sea unalterably behind him, so too the ghost of Christie O'Brien had retreated far into the depths of his awareness. If Christie had somewhat controlled the thoughts of the boy, Seagull commanded the full attention of the man.

With Raymondo and Calling Owl at the shingle mill encampment to oversee that operation, and with the redoubtable Sam Flowers seeing to it that the Branciforte men were kept well-occupied with broad axe, adze, drawknife, and shingling hatchet, Beard and his new wife rode northward to Butano Ridge and Pescadero Creek— partly to gain familiarity with the locations of the groves of redwoods and partly just to have some time to themselves. From Beard's point of view, at least, the bustle and closeness of both Hotochruk village and the logging camp were simply too confining. When a man was in love, after all, that man was surely entitled to some privacy. He and Seagull had some . . . well . . . *exploring* to do.

Below the oak and brush-covered rim of Butano Ridge, Bill Beard and Seagull came down into a gully where mountain laurel, bush lupines, and hemlocks grew in profusion. There were small hanging gardens of grass and fern as well, and from under a sheaf of layered sandstone a considerable spring flowed, jumping on down the mountainside amidst spates of sunlight and making its way into a heavy grove of large redwoods and fir trees several hundred feet below where the husband and wife sat their ponies.

"The sun will soon go down behind the ocean fog," Seagull said. "Tonight's sky will burn red. Let us camp here, high on the mountain. It will be much warmer than down below. On the ridges there are always warm breezes after dark."

Beard nodded.

"Cold air sinks," he said. "You're right, Gull. We could hardly find a nicer place to . . . make a baby."

Seagull laughed.

"I'm not like most Hotochruk women," she replied as her husband moved here and there, gathering chunks of dry limbwood. "I have no desire for children. I've watched the others. Little ones are a great deal of bother."

"*Hostages to fortune.*" Beard laughed.

"What does that mean?"

"Nothing, I suppose. Something Francis Bacon said—an Englishman, yep, a long time ago."

"Is this *Baking* someone you and Raymondo have met in Monterey?"

"No. Bacon's dead—many many seasons ago. But I've read some of the things he wrote—published in books. He was a great writer, a very important man."

"Will you write a book one day, my husband? That way others could read about how my father captured you and how, when he gave you your freedom, I captured you a second time. People could read about how we built a fire here on the mountainside and cooked our dinner and then—"

Seagull began to laugh.

"If I wrote such a book," Beard said, "how in the devil would you know what I said in it? How would you know I told the truth?"

"Because you have promised to teach me how to read. Have you forgotten your promise? I wish to be able to read Raymondo's *Quixote* book myself."

"Sure enough, Gull. We'll start those reading lessons . . . tomorrow. Tonight's for making love."

Beard dismounted and helped his wife down from her pony. Then he turned the animals to graze—watched as the horses trotted over to the rivulet, drank hugely from a rock-lined basin, and began to gather green grass into their mouths.

Already a soft, warm wind was rising from the basin of Pescadero Creek. The air was rich with the redolent, intermingled odors of laurel and fir resin and aromatic chaparral.

They cooked some chewy biscuits made of acorn meal, as well as slices of young wild pig meat (the previous afternoon Sam Flowers, company hunter and unofficial *booshway*, had brought into the logging camp the gutted-out carcasses of four of the unfortunate creatures, along with a big doe and a fat boar raccoon). They sipped at Mexican wine as they ate and listened to the trills of screech owls off in the darkness. To the west the night sky came rich with stars, though in all likelihood fog would drift in off the ocean before morning, while to the east a moon past full drifted skyward across the long, irregularly-shaped forms of the Santa Cruz Mountains.

"I will tell you a story," Seagull said. "Do you wish to listen?"

Beard chewed off a chunk of pork and grinned, the juice trickling down onto his beard.

"I'd be charmed, lady, charmed. What's this yarn you've got in mind?"

"There are many storytellers among the Ohlones," Seagull smiled. "Calling Owl and I have always listened well to the old ones. One day we will also be old, and then the young ones will listen to us perhaps."

Beard sipped wine and passed the skin to Gull.

"An old Yokuts man came to live with us several winters ago. He stayed with us one season, and then he went to Other Side Camp. The Yokuts live beyond the inland water, across the mountains were the great valley is very flat and very wide. A big river runs through that valley, and that's where this old man once lived. But when his wife died, he left his people and began to wander. He wandered until some of my father's warriors found him living in a death lodge not far from where we are right now. The young men convinced him to accompany them back to Hotochruk. After that he became friends with Pelican Doctor. He lived alone, but he liked children and often would tell stories. I wish he were still alive. . . ."

"Death is the human condition, the ultimate fate," Beard replied. "Perhaps one day someone will discover an elixir that'll allow us to live forever. It would be strange to live so long—to watch things changing. I think these hills will melt down to the sea eventually."

"No," Seagull said, snuggling against Beard's shoulder, "that's not what will happen. The mountains came out of the sea, long ago. That's why there are seashells in the rocks. I think maybe they will become even higher. Probably we could find some shells right over there, above the spring."

"Perhaps, perhaps. So what's this story you wanted to tell?"

Seagull took a deep breath and then began.

"I think the old man was telling his own story," she said, "for his wife had died, and I think he loved her very much. They had been many years together. This is his story:

"A man had a wife, and she was a good woman. But then she died, and he was all alone. They had never had any children. If he'd had children, he might have wished to live for them—just as Pelican Doctor did when our mother died. But now this Yokuts man burned his hair and covered himself with slimy mud from a creek bank. He stayed by his wife's grave day and night, and he refused to eat. He smoked his pipe, but didn't drink or eat at all. He didn't even sleep, because he knew his wife's spirit would leave the grave, and Yokuts Man intended to follow her to the land of the dead.

"Then Yokuts Woman sat up in her grave, and the loose dirt fell away from her. She went down to the stream and cleansed herself, and then she put her skirt, apron, and beads back on. She tied her hair with a band of fox fur—and all the while she acted as though she did not even see her poor husband. When he came to her and tried to embrace her, his arms passed right through her body. She slipped away. But Yokuts Man had a rope made from milkweed down, and he put this about her waist. Holding to this cord, he was able to follow her all through the night as she walked ahead toward the land of the dead.

"When dawn came, the wife became invisible. She rested, because the dead only travel at night. Yokuts Woman was a ghost, and yet she left footprints in the loose earth. The husband could see these. He watched them to make sure she had not left him behind.

"When night came again, Yokuts Man felt the tug on the milkweed down cord, and once more he followed her. For four days and nights this pattern was repeated, and during all this time the husband did not sleep, did not eat, did not drink. He loved his wife so deeply that he had to be with her. He could not bring himself to live without her."

"I've read a story just like this one," Beard said, musing. "Perhaps all people have such a story. The details are different, but . . . Orpheus and Eurydice . . . a very, very old tale."

"You will tell me if your story is exactly the same, then. In this tale," Seagull continued, "the darkness came again, and now the wife turned to her husband and asked why he kept following her. He replied that he loved her and didn't wish to live without her. He intended to follow her to the land of the dead, if that were necessary. But she said that he couldn't do that—it wasn't possible. Yokuts Woman said the way would become ever more dangerous for him, even though it was safe for her—since she was dead.

"Then he said, *I will go with you to the land of the dead people. If it is possible, I will bring you away from there. If it's not possible, then I'll remain with you.* But she said, *It isn't possible. You must understand, my husband, I am nothing at all now. You wish to make love to me, but I am no longer able to do such a thing. I have no body to give you.* And he replied, *No matter. Love is more than what the body is able to do. Yet I will be able to bring you back, even back to your body, because I am determined. I use the power of my mind. Because of my love for you, my mind has grown very strong.*

"Yokuts Woman could see that nothing she said would deter her husband. He had always been very brave and also very stubborn. She led onward, down into a very deep canyon whose walls were sheer stone. At the bottom a river was in flood, its dark waters roaring and churning through its chasm. Great boulders crashed back and forth, and Yokuts Woman feared her husband would be crushed between them. The boulders could not harm her, however, because her body was gone—she had left her bones in the grave.

"Yokuts Man said a prayer. He clung to the milkweed down cord and dashed between the boulders. For a long while he lay there, resting, and his wife waited for him. Then they continued their journey, following the river down to where it emptied into a big blue lake. There were many lodges clustered among the meadows close by the lake's shore, and a bridge made of woven grass rope spanned the river so that travelers might enter into the land of the dead. Beside this bridge sat a man with the face of a hawk—a guardian who explained to Yokuts Man that despite his prayers and his determination, some of the dead would resent his presence. They would not wish to have a living person among them, for they would not think it appropriate.

"Yokuts Man held to the milkweed down cord and followed his wife across the swaying bridge. Sea gulls flew at him and tried to peck out his eyes, but he shielded his face with one hand and fought to retain his balance. Finally they made it all the way across and stepped into the land of the dead."

"You sure it was *sea gulls*?" Beard asked. "I'd have thought *eagles* or *vultures*. . . ."

"Perhaps the old man meant *demon birds*," Seagull said. "Perhaps he was just playing a joke on me—because of my name. He was a very funny man—like a joking uncle. Are you listening my husband? Now the man and the wife had reached the land of the dead, and here they met

Coyote Man himself. Part of the time Coyote is chief of the dead people. Coyote asked Yokuts Woman who the man was, and she said, *My husband. He's still alive, but he insisted on coming with me. . . .*

"Coyote Man sent Yokuts Woman on to join the other dead people, and he asked Yokuts Man why he had made so dangerous a journey. *Because I love my wife and do not wish to live without her,* he said.

"Coyote felt sorry for the husband and sent him down to bathe. After that he gave Yokuts Man food and drink. Then Coyote spoke: *You should never have come here, my friend. You are brave, but how can I help you? You must go back to your village until the time comes for you to die. Then you may join your wife. For now, stay with us a time. You will see how it is. The dead will not wish you to be around them, since they will suppose you stink, like someone with a bad stomach. In any case, don't try to sleep with Yokuts Woman. Remember that she is dead and cannot do as you may wish.*

"When evening came and the fires were lit everywhere, Yokuts Man stayed at a distance from the others and watched what they did. Only by darkness were the spirits of the dead visible to him. There, sitting around one campfire, were many of his own relatives—those who had died in the flooding river a year earlier and those who had died of the coughing disease. He also saw friends whom he had known long ago, when he was a boy. Some were playing the stick game, and he wished to join them. Then men and women left their fires and moved to the dancing area and began to dance. Some used conch shells to chant a song, and others clicked stones together or slapped at deerskin drums. Even his own wife played the stick game with the other women, and after that she began to dance. When dawn finally came, the others went away, but Yokuts Woman came back to where her unhappy husband was sitting, alone. As soon as the daylight arrived, however, he could no longer see her.

"They talked all day—the man and the spirit of his wife, even though he could not see her. When darkness returned and she appeared once again, he tied to fondle her

breasts and to entice her to lie down with him. But as soon
as he took her into his arms, he fell deeply asleep. He did
not wake up until after Yokuts Woman had gone off to dance
with her dead friends. . . ."

"Listen!" Bill Beard whispered, pushing Seagull from
him and rising. He withdrew his Hudson's Bay fusee from
the tie-down leg holster in which he carried the weapon and
stared out into darkness.

The riding ponies began to nicker and, almost on cue,
a   spotted   owl   gave   its   distinctive   barking
sound—*whooo-whooo-whooo-whooaah*. . . .

"Gull! Get behind the tree—there's someone
close. . . ."

"Why would anyone be here on the mountain?"

"Don't know. Keep down. I'll be right back. . . ."

Beard, crouching, moved quickly to the edge of the
firelight, listened intently, allowed his vision to adjust to
the moonlit darkness.

He was aware of something—something or someone—
close. He even supposed he could detect the sound of
breathing—and an odor, slightly rancid, suggestive of de-
caying flesh. Perhaps downslope a deer lay dead; yes, and
vultures, feeding, were at the same time fanning their big
wings.

"Vultures roost at night. Daytime's for feeding. . . ."

Again the *whooo-whooo-whooo-whooaah!* of the spotted owl.

Beard, pistol still in hand and its hammer set, turned
abruptly and strode back to the fire. From a saddlebag
slung over an oak limb, he withdrew a makeshift torch,
pulled off its leathern hood, and doused the wire-bound
cotton wicking with whale oil.

"Bill, what is it?" Seagull demanded.

"Damned if I know. Stay where you are—keep down.
Possibly we're being visited by a hunting party from
Tamie-n village. Aren't they the people who live on Coyote
River? In any case, that's the only village close enough to
us. . . ."

Beard dipped his torch into the open flames of the

small fire pit, and the odor of burning whale oil carried on the night air. Torch in one hand and fusee in the other, he walked calmly out to where he'd previously stood.

"Whoever's there," he called out, "declare yourselves! What is your business? *Hileu ma tanim*, where are you going? *Quien passa?*"

The silence was broken only by the sounds of the nervous dashing about of quail in the brush.

"Are you *tumas-hachohpa*, the night spirit?" Beard persisted. "Show yourself!"

Then a section of downed log heaved itself upright, and Beard's torch clearly outlined the massive body and face of a bear. The creature opened its mouth as though to display its impressive teeth, and the odor of rotten flesh was even more pronounced. Beard was obliged to force himself to hold his ground. The huge creature was a grizzly, not a harmless black bear. A single swipe of one of those forearms, Beard knew, would likely be sufficient to sever his head from his shoulders or to crush in his skull. A shot from the fusee might or might not accomplish anything. Clearly, if a first shot did not drop the beast, there would be no time to reload and fire a second time. In such an event, his hunting knife would prove his only weapon.

"Go away, old friend!" Seagull said, her voice firm and full of authority. "We wish you no harm."

She was standing beside him now, light from the torch seeming to trickle down through her long, braided hair.

"Gull, I told ye to stay back. . . ."

"Take this food and go," Seagull continued.

She tossed the remainder of the acorn flour biscuit at the grizzly's feet.

The huge creature uttered a *huff-huff-hock* sound, dropped to all fours, and took the chunk of biscuit in its mouth. Turning about, the bear moved off into the night, its footfalls hardly heard, its motion astonishingly fluid and even graceful.

Bill Beard shook his head and began to laugh—the deep laughter of profound relief.

"Friend of yours?" he asked.

"Perhaps," Seagull replied. "All the animals are friendly enough—even the grizzly, most of the time at least. They have bad tempers. It isn't their fault. I don't think they can help themselves. So it is that they kill somebody once in a while. But I think that happens only when they are challenged in some way—or when the mother attempts to protect her young. The mothers can be very fierce."

"Have to admit," Beard said, "I'd a hell of a lot rather feed that old brute than have a fistfight with him."

"No one should attempt to fistfight with the grizzly," Seagull insisted. "Not even Coyote Man can control the golden bear. He doesn't try. Either he leaves the grizzly alone, or he outwits him and then keeps his distance. Probably there's nothing in the world that a grizzly's afraid of."

Beard cast a last glance downslope, into the darkness where the brute, chewing baked acorn mush, had disappeared. Then he sheathed his fusee and put his one free arm about Seagull's waist. The two of them walked back to their fire. Beard did not extinguish his torch. Rather, he propped it between two sheafs of chalkstone, took a long pull from the wineskin, heaped wood on the fire, sat down beside Seagull, lit his pipe, and puffed contentedly for a few moments.

Yet again the spotted owl barked: *whooo-whooo-whooo-whoaah!*

"Old Griz could well have been the chief of the dead people," Beard said. "I know you said that role belonged to Coyote Man, but I'd say the big bear ought to be given some consideration."

"There are often several versions of one story. Perhaps for another tale-teller the grizzly was the one. But I will finish the way the old Yokuts had it. Do you remember where I was when you heard the bear shuffling around in the brush?"

"Yokuts Man tried to fondle his wife, and then he went

to sleep. She left him and went away to dance with the dead people."

Seagull nodded.

"Yes. To dance and play in one of the games. Just before the sun came up, Yokuts Woman returned to her husband, and once again they talked all day. The husband did not think of sleeping, even though he was still alive and could not live without it. I think it is necessary for us to dream, and that is why we must sleep. Finally the sun went down, and Yokuts Man thought about putting his little horn, his *shikid*, into his wife's body. As soon as he tried to do this, however, he once more fell fast asleep, and so Yokuts Woman went off to dance and to play the stick game and the hand game.

"At last Coyote Man came to the husband and said, *Since you are determined to mate with your wife, you must leave the land of the dead. The spirits do not believe it is right that a living person should be among them—since you always wish to do the things that living people do*.

"But Coyote Man felt sorry for this human who had left his own life behind in order to come with his woman. Perhaps never before had a man loved his wife so dearly— even more dearly than life itself. His devotion to her had made Yokuts Woman cherish him even more than when she had been a living person, making love to her husband and taking him inside her body. She had told Coyote Man that she would be willing to return with Yokuts Man to the world of the living, if that were possible. While she knew it was not the way of nature for a spirit woman to live in the lodge of a man who still had his flesh and bones, she realized that he loved her so much that he could not live without her. Later they would both return, for that is the fate of all. Coyote Man agreed, but it was necessary for him to provide one condition. He spoke to the husband and said: *Your trip back to the village where you lived before will take you six days and six nights. For that length of time, Yokuts Man, you must not touch your wife in the way of man and woman. You must not fondle her breasts or attempt to lie down with her—no, not even just to sleep in one another's arms. Being that close together often causes both the man and the woman to become excited, and after that they will always wish to mate with one another. Not even great willpower is sufficient to prevent them.*

"Yokuts Man was very happy," Seagull continued, "and he agreed to the condition Coyote Man had set. Immediately the husband and his wife started their journey—across the bridge where the birds flew about like angry insects and then up the flooding river and then across between the giant rocks that crushed against one another. Beyond that lay the long trail that led back to their country. When at last the land became familiar to them, they knew they would reach their home village in just one more day.

"When darkness came and Yokuts Man could once more see his wife, he was overcome with desire for her. He told Yokuts Woman that he could wait no longer—that his desire was a terrible ache and would drive him crazy if she did not help him to do something about it. *My husband,* Yokuts Woman insisted, *you heard what Coyote Man told us. We must not do anything to make him angry, for then he would change his mind and take back what he has given us.* For a long while Yokuts Man lay there on his back, moaning and groaning. His wife was sorry for him, and she reached over to hold him—just as she might have held the child she had never borne to him. When she touched his manhood, he began to cry with desire. He could wait no longer. He had fasted and prayed and gone without drink for many days, and now all his desire had to be satisfied."

"That's the end of the story?" Beard demanded. "I think I'm going to do to you just what Yokuts Man did to Yokuts Woman. . . ."

"I hoped you would want to do that," Seagull said, her voice grown somewhat husky. "But there is still more to the story."

"We're near to the end, I hope? I'm starting to have a little problem myself."

"I will make it into a bigger problem for you, *Señor Hair on the Face,* but first I must finish the story."

"Hurry then, Gull, for God's sake. . . ."

"Yes. This is how the tale ends. When Yokuts Man entered his wife's body, she disappeared. She vanished. Even though it was still nighttime, he could not see her after that. The next day a group of young warriors from the village came running along this particular trail, and then suddenly they stopped. Here they found Yokuts Man. He was lying there, facedown on the road that led from the place where Yokuts Woman was buried to the village. Yokuts Man's arms were outstretched, and his heart had gone away. He was dead."

Beard puffed on his pipe, nodded.

"He had gone back to the land of the dead? Now he was also a ghost, and so it was possible for him to join her there?"

"Perhaps that is so," Seagull agreed. "Perhaps that is so, if Coyote Man was willing to allow it. It is wrong to grieve too much for one who has died, but maybe if one loves enough, then such grief is permitted."

12

Wild Goose Chase

Beard and Olivo left their operation on the San Lorenzo and rode south to Villa de Branciforte, where they were able to transact some minor business, among other things making arrangements for half a dozen additional men to go to work a couple of weeks hence. In addition, they were able to acquire a pair of Mexican army pistols of relatively recent vintage. Beard made a point of not asking how the weapons had fallen into the possession of the proprietor of La Cantina.

Transactions completed, the partners skirted the hills above Santa Cruz, not hurrying in the slightest, enjoying the pleasant early California autumn. By this time of the year in Vermont, Bill told Raymondo, water troughs would be frozen each morning, while the oaks, hickories, elms, and white-barked willows would already have begun their riotous display of colors.

In Alta California, however, daytime temperatures were, if anything, slightly higher than had been the case at midsummer. Some oaks were of a mind to remain verdant all winter, while even the maples showed no more than faint traces of yellow.

Bill and Raymondo discussed various matters as they rode, including the increasing reliance they were already placing upon the abilities of Samson Flowers, the twenty-seven-year-old former and perhaps future mountain man, trapper, and sometime sojourner to the continent's dark interior.

"In the long run, I don't think Señor Flowers will prove to be a very good cutter of shingles," Raymondo said. "In San José, I have seen men like him before. They come and then they go. He's a big, strong fellow, and he's full of bluster, but I don't think him to be very responsible. At one time I believed you to be such a man as well, Sancho Bill. *No obstante*, I can see that you seem to like Flowers, though I'm not certain we should have hired him at all."

Bill shrugged.

"Hell's bells, Pontiff, you've got to give us Americans a proper chance, that's all. Flowers taught you to shoe horses, and I turned out okay, didn't I?"

"*Sí, sí, mediano. . . .*"

Beard had led with his chin. He knew it.

"Ray, it's obvious Flowers has the respect of his fellow *bandidos*. He doesn't strike me as a logger, either. Perhaps it's best if we just designate him *cahuna* and camp hunter—cook as well, if he'll go for it."

"It's possible he might be a good foreman—if we needed such a person," Raymondo reflected. "Perhaps you're right. Who am I to judge? At the moment, however, you and I must return to Hotochruk to visit our wives. Already they doubtlessly languish without us. At least that must be so in the case of Calling Owl. Do not suppose, Sancho Beard, that because I am short and do not have hair all over my face that I lack either information or skill in the matter of lovemaking. It's quality, quality that counts. And that's why Calling Owl has always about her face a certain *satisfied* expression. As for the unfortunate Seagull, why, who can say? Besides, we must be careful to keep Pelican Doctor's goodwill. The chief knew nothing of any plan to bring these men—criminals and misfits, that is what they are—into his territory. He wasn't completely pleased when we told him."

Bill laughed.

"Such a description fits you and me just as well, Señor Quixote, man of few words. You're right, naturally."

"*A todas luces*, obviously."

Bill and Raymondo, trailing a pack animal, made their way to the coast road, and once there, they immediately drew up their mounts. Apparently a good deal of traffic had preceded them northward, and probably not by more than a few hours—men on horseback and several wagons as well.

"*Clemente Dios!* The Leather Jackets! What other explanation can there be? Bill, I think Patrón Diego is on his way to attack Hotochruk. Perhaps it's too late even to get a warning to Pelican Doctor. I've told you what has happened to some Ohlone villages. . . ."

Scenes of massacre flashed through both minds—lodges burning, dead lying strewn about in the meadow near the two great redwood trees. Seagull and Calling Owl—taken prisoner by Leather Jackets, raped, humiliated.

Blind rage ran through Beard. He'd been so utterly intent upon founding a business, succeeding in the best Yankee fashion in this foreign land, that he'd all but failed to consider the situation of those strange, gentle children of the forest—among them the woman he loved dearly, the woman he'd taken to wife, Seagull. . . .

Bill detected a stricken expression on Raymondo's face—realized it was but the mirror image of his own.

"Our woodcutters have weapons," Bill said. "They have no love for the authorities, but they're willing to do as we say only because we pay them well. Do you think they'd be willing to engage the Gawd-cursed Leather Jackets if necessary?"

Raymondo checked the load in his pistol, nodded.

"Perhaps that will work," he said. "Ride to our *campamento* as quickly as your horse will carry you. That is best. I will go directly to Hotochruk. If a battle's in progress, then I'll join in. If the soldiers have already struck, then I'll wait for you to arrive. We'll bury our dead and then pursue vengeance."

"It's all crazy, crazy!" Beard said. "But worth a try. The men will follow Flowers, some of them at least, even if they won't follow us. We have to do something. We can cut over the mountain and come down by Stone Face Falls. Surely the soldiers won't attack until tomorrow—if indeed this Patrón Lopez Diego is able to find Pelican Doctor's village. We know where it is because we've lived there. But the Patrón will have to search everywhere. . . . Gawddamn it, Raymondo, don't you go getting yourself killed, now!"

They rode in different directions. Bill pushed on well into the night, sounded the dinner gong directly upon reaching the encampment, and then proceeded to heap tinder upon the coals of the watchfire.

Flowers emerged from his cowhide tent, a long knife in one hand, while on his face was the expression of a man who had in mind to slit someone's throat. The others, yawning and cursing perfunctorily, grudgingly stood in a semicircle near the fire.

Bill explained the situation as he saw it and offered a bonus to any man who was willing to assist an Indian village under attack by the Mexican regulars.

"Damned right these lads is ready to fight if they has to." Samson Flowers laughed. "Most of us was jest sitting there in Branchy-fort waiting for something excitin' to happen, only it never did, until them Gord-cursed Leather Jackets come bustin' in and clapped some of our fellows into chains, an' then you an' Raymondo hauled our ashes out hyar to butcher trees. Ain't that we love Injuns especially, ye understand, not on principle at least, but we sure as hell don't think much of them stiff-back Meskin soldiers. Lead on, Gen'ral! We'll plant the lot o' them under some buckeye brush! Cain't let that Olivo fight the Meskins all by hisself, can we?"

With Samson Flowers and the rest of the men in tow, Bill led the small Army of the Republic across the intervening ridges to Stone Face Falls in the canyon of *Riachuelo*

Grande. Smoke hung in the air, and a tearing pain hit Beard, as real as though he'd been stabbed with the machete that Flowers carried.

Flowers sidled his big mule next to Bill's horse.

"Señor Beard, this Injun village we're lookin' for—I take it she's down-canyon. You figger the Meskin regulars has beat us to it?"

·"How could they have known where . . . ?" Beard asked no one in particular, his voice trailing off on a note of stoic acceptance.

Maybe someone followed our trail that last trip up the coast. We imagined we were looking out for the safety of Pelican Doctor's people, when in fact we must have led one of the patrón's scouts right to Hotochruk—close enough, at least, so he could figure out just where it was. . . .

"The soldiers could have circled over the north canyon wall—looked right down on the village itself. . . ."

"Con-jecture, by Gord, con-jecture," Flowers replied. "The truth is, we don't know for certain what's happened yet. Injuns is always settin' the woods on fire this time of year. We don't know the Meskins actually come up this canyon, do we? Guess we ought to go look."

Beard nodded. Flowers, he couldn't help thinking, had a certain canny wisdom that was far beyond his twenty-seven years. Samson had been, in fact, as much a wanderer as he had—but on horseback or muleback rather than aboard various merchant vessels. He'd fought against such tribes as the Blackfeet and the Klamats. In any case, under the present circumstances, Bill felt inclined to follow Samson's lead and to trust his instincts.

Bill took a deep breath and urged his horse forward.

They reached the creek just below the falls and proceeded downstream. As they approached the site of Hotochruk village, smoke lay much heavier, and the cause was not difficult to discover. Hotochruk had been burned—its lodges, all of them, overthrown and set ablaze, though by now the flames had died back. Fire worked its way down-canyon under the influence of wind from the Santa Cruz Mountains, jumped the creek, and was presently stuttering along in an irregular band through thin cover on the steep canyonside.

Raymondo was there, waiting, his swarthy face a virtual death mask.

No Leather Jackets were in sight, and neither were there any Indian bodies lying about—what Beard deeply feared and had already accepted, as a way of preparing himself for the worst. In the open meadow, strips of drying meat and fish still hung on the racks, and a number of watertight baskets filled with soaking acorns stood in an irregular row close by the mortar stones and the stream.

Flowers dismounted immediately and studied the earthen area of what had been just a day earlier the central circle of Hotochruk.

"Meskins been here all right," he said, no particular expression on his face. "From the looks o' things, I'd guess the Injuns must of lit out up the canyon wall, knowing the Leather Jackets would figure ponies couldn't make 'er. If the soldiers was goin' to follow, they'd likely have tried it from the other side—next canyon over. . . ."

Raymondo gritted his teeth, spat.

"Then they would have to understand the *terreno*. They know just how to track down their prey."

"No dead Hotochrukma here," Bill said. "Somehow Pelican Doctor got them all out—the wounded too, if there were any. More likely, though, a village scout caught sight of the Leather Jackets in time and came running back to the lodges. The Hotochrukma move through the forest as quietly as deer, and they know every rim and arroyo by heart. As a matter of fact, horses aren't going to be any great advantage to Patrón Lopez Diego, not if you ask this Vermont Yankee."

"If you're still of a mind to help out," Flowers said as he swung back into the saddle, "then let's get a move on. . . ."

Olivo was outraged with the injustice and the senselessness of the whole business.

"*Jesus y Papa*, what if we meet the Leather Jackets before we catch up with Pelican Doctor? Not even the maimed Cervantes himself would know what is the right thing to do. . . ."

Flowers reached forward to scratch his mule between the ears. The creature fluttered its lips in appreciation.

"That's easy." Flowers grinned. "Gents, what we do then is . . . we help 'em find your Injun friends, only we do it in sich a way that the chief, he gets off clean an' clear, by Gord. At least he will if he's any kind o' chief at all. You fellows know these hills pretty good, as I take it? Cap'm Lopez Diablo, he's never been this far north before. Hails out of San Gabriel, or so I'm told."

"Diego," Bill said. "*El Diablo*, that's the Devil."

"One an' the same, Mr. Beard. Half o' one an' six dozen o' the other. Never could tell the difference between a Meskin officer and one o' Scratch's men."

Raymondo laughed. "Don Quixote himself would be proud of such a plan. We pretend to be patriots who have ridden out to join the fun. But our men, Señor Flowers, are these not some of the same ones for whom the Patrón Diego brought arrest warrants into Branciforte?"

"Sure enough, including this coondog hisself. Wouldn't recognize me, though. I expect Diablo'll take whatever help he can get—and be grateful into the bargain. In the meanwhile, gents, I'd appreciate it if ye'd just call me Jim-Bob. Sort of uncomplicates things for the cap'm, and keeps my neck from gettin' any longer than it is. Truth is, it was time for me to head on out of Branciforte anyhow. I needed a grubstake so's I could mosey on back to beaver country, and a season o' logging and shingle-chopping should do it. Let's get a move on now, that's what I say."

Some have believed Fate to be even more powerful than the gods themselves, as was the case with Homer's carefree and blundering Argive warriors and also with Pelican Doctor's people of the forest. The Great Dreamer dreams for a time, and then he awakens and instructs World Maker or Coyote to shift things about somewhat. Fate was clearly at work, adjusting the affairs of Beard and Olivo that happy moment when Samson Flowers was taken into their employ—and the same had been true of the more-or-less chance meeting with Jean Paul Martin, who was to prove both their angel and their commercial outlet to the rest of the world.

As Bill was to learn subsequently, Patrón Diego had been given the assignment of eliminating, if possible, the last few pockets of resistance to governmental authority in the Santa Cruz-Monterey area. In truth, the man's heart was not in his work, for though Imperial Spain was his nominal employer, there was very little in the way of *hidalgo* blood in his veins. His essential lineage was Toltec, and his sympathies were clearly with Mexico. On that fortunate day when Mexico threw off Spanish shackles, should such ever happen, men like Diego (from far Yucatan to Alta California) would quietly shift allegiance, find superior officers to salute, and be about their business.

Patrón Diego and his Leather Jackets had approached Hotochruk from the south, moving on horseback down through a heavy stand of redwoods and firs and brush, thus creating rather considerable noise and commotion. By the time the soldiers were within sight of the Ohlone village, the Hotochrukma were on the move, scrambling up various trails along the more barren northern slope. The Leather Jackets attempted to ride out into the meadow, but arrows began to sing about their ears. One soldier was shot through the forearm, and another arrow embedded itself into a horse's rump.

The Leather Jackets pulled back and began to fire at the escaping Indians, but with indeterminate success. The patrón thought it likely that several Indians had been wounded, at the very least.

Once the troops took possession of the deserted village, Diego ordered the lodges torched. Realizing the Ohlones were without horses, however, and for this reason able to take an escape route that his men, on their mounts, could not immediately follow, Diego ordered the soldiers down-canyon and then northward in what he presumed to be hot pursuit of the elusive Hotochrukma. Reaching a low

divide between drainages, the patrón then turned his
Leather Jackets inland along a wide, sloping crest that led
ultimately to the spine of the Santa Cruz Range.

It was at this point, some fifteen miles or more from
the site of the burned village below Stone Face Falls, that
Olivo and Beard and their men came within hailing distance
of the Mexican-Spanish soldiers.

William Beard, carrying a white flag so as not to have
his intentions misunderstood, cantered his mount forward
in order to speak with Lopez Diego.

Bill offered his assistance, and it was accepted gra-
ciously. The patrón had with him no more than twenty
men, three of whom had been severely wounded. Several
hours earlier some band of Indians, presumably members
of the target group whose village Diego had already
torched, counterattacked, opening fire from ambush—a
great surprise to the patrón, though he'd been repeatedly
advised that Pelican Doctor's people had at least a few
firearms.

In any case, no one was killed, and the encounter was
brief indeed. As a matter of fact, the patrón informed
Beard, the savages vanished back into the fir glades almost
as though they possessed the capacity to become incorpo-
real.

Flowers and Olivo rode up beside them, and after
some discussion with the officer, agreement was made to
lead him and his troops northward—for Samson Flowers,
a.k.a. Jim-Bob, insisted that he'd once spent a week with
Pelican Doctor's boys as an unwilling guest, and that their
secret hideaway was beyond the rims of the mountains and
within view of Bahía del San Francisco.

After talking with Beard and Olivo a bit longer and
being assured that they indeed knew their way about these
mountains, Diego dispatched Cabo Dominguez and four
other able-bodied men to return to Santa Cruz with the
wounded. This matter attended to, the patrón and a dozen
of his men, as well as Raymondo and Bill and Samson and
the eleven other employees rode off toward the north,

making careful investigation of various thicketed gullies along the way and finally cresting the range once again.

There, on the lee slope, they found plentiful grass for the animals and running water as well—for a respectable spring was bubbling from beneath a shelf of stone on the hillside.

With heavy cloudbars to the westward already turning toward an orange and scarlet sundown, they encamped for the night.

Jim-Bob suggested the wisdom of two all-night guards, one above and one below, these to be taken half shift each by a pair of soldiers. The *Chuckers*, as he called Pelican Doctor's people, were particularly vicious after dark—and in fact were commonly known to sneak into civilized pueblos and slit men's throats for no reason beyond the pure fun of it.

Diego nodded without real conviction and ordered his men to take turns at the watch. Bill and Raymondo noted that the Leather Jackets weren't in the least inclined to volunteer participation. Flowers had the appearance of a man genuinely pleased with himself. He sniffed the air, squinted westward toward the last remnants of sunset, and informed one and all that they should anticipate rain within an hour or two.

Raymondo agreed.

"It is coming," he said. "I too can feel its presence."

Indeed, before the last of the four cooking fires had been reduced to a heap of glowing coals, drops of moisture began to hiss down from out of the night.

Exhausted, Bill fell into a deep sleep, a slumber that was blessedly without dreams of any sort—no images of the wounded and the dying—no images of burials—of wailings and gnashings of teeth.

At first light a few notes from a *corneta de llaves* floated through a salt-smelling drizzle. The Leather Jackets were almost immediately up and about, even those two unfortunate individuals who'd kept late watch and whose uniforms were, for that reason, quite soggy. Flowers managed to roust the crew of would-be and actual timber beasts.

After a quick, cold breakfast of tortillas and beans, the men disconsolate beneath chilly gray skies, the group continued its search, dropping down into a long, narrow, trenchlike valley lying on a north-south axis—the valley of San Andreas, according to Diego's poorly drawn chart. Here they made note of several places that seemed to indicate recent earth movement, banks, and in one instance even a well-traveled wagon trail offset by some three to four feet, with a result that a strange little right-left-right jag in the roadway had been worn into place.

"It's one of those spots," Raymondo mused, "where Coyote rubs part of the earth against another. There are many such places in this land of ours, and that's why sometimes the ground shakes beneath our feet. This is the actual reason, señors, and not simply that a great tree has fallen in the night."

The patrón, however, wasn't concerned with geological theorizings, and since *terra firma* was being just that at the moment (albeit occasionally mud-slick), without comment he directed his men on past this zone of dislocation. Upon reaching the far ridge crest, Diego split his troop, half to proceed northward and half southward, the whole to reassemble in four hours' time upon this same spot.

Though thus enabled to double the area of their futile search for the Ohlones, neither party made any further contact with Pelican Doctor and his people. By the time the light rainstorm had fairly well dissipated and blue patches were beginning to appear overhead, the two groups were reassembled. At the patrón's direction, they then proceeded to a small round valley cupped in the oak and scrub-pine-covered hills of the inland slope, to what had apparently been an Ohlone village at some time in the not too distant past.

At this very location Jim-Bob asserted once again that he'd been held captive by the *red divvils* and would likely have been flayed alive (a commonly inflicted Indian torture, according to Flowers) had not a doe-eyed, nubile little maiden of perhaps thirteen summers taken a shine to him and, on the sly, cut his bonds—thus allowing him to flee on foot, barefoot and indeed without any clothing at all, until he was able to take refuge in a cave which he was obliged to share with a mother grizzly and three cubs. Flowers was just about to begin a discourse on the inherently superior flavor and nutrient powers of grizzly milk when Beard jabbed him in the ribs and brought his tale to an abrupt conclusion.

The patrón, fortunately, had ceased to pay any attention to Jim-Bob—at about the point in the tale where the lovely young Ohlone maiden decided inexplicably to set him free.

"You and me, Señor Jim-Bob," Raymondo said in a low voice and with as straight a face as he could muster, "we will write a book together. I myself will provide the narrative elements, and you will invent the incidents necessary to the telling of the tale. Perhaps we will call this epic *The Life and Times of Sam Flowers, Knight Errant.*"

Samson grinned, nodded.

"Good idee, damned good idee," he replied.

In the meanwhile, Patrón Lopez Diego dismounted and strutted about the area, examining in cursory fashion several stone-inlaid lodge sites. The Leather Jacket captain briskly mounted his horse, gave a signal to move forward, and resumed lead position, bringing the group down to evening bivouac close by El Camino Real, that grandiloquently-titled wagon route along the western shore of the Bay of San Francisco, the main road, such as it was, from San José to Yerba Buena.

Just at red sundown arrows streamed into the encampment, wounding several of Lopez Diego's troops and two Olivo & Beard loggers as well. Men dived for whatever cover presented itself and began to fire at shadows. Horses reared and lashed out with their hooves. The patrón shouted orders and then inexplicably drew his sword and strode directly into the center of the confusion.

"Get down, ye damned fool!" Flowers yelled—and then, realizing the patrón could not hear him and was in any case in the midst of a confused attempt to determine just what in the hell was happening, Samson leaped up from behind a downfall cedar and dashed to the officer's side.

"Jim-Bob, *esta lloviendo*, it is raining arrows. . . ."

"Ye tryin' to get kilt, man? We been lookin' for Pelican Doctor, an' now we've found him. He's got us pinned down an' in a crossfire to boot. Get hold of yourself. Ain't just arrows comin' down. Them Injuns has Gorddamn well got flintlocks. . . ."

An arrow struck the earth no more than three feet from where the Leather Jacket officer was standing, skidded along the wet earth, spun end for end.

"Could of stuck in one o' us," Flowers noted.

Diego glared at the American, recognized the wisdom of what had been said, and followed Flowers toward meager cover of a growth of young California laurel.

"Cease fire, *basta! Basta*, damn you!" Diego's voice rang out.

"Calm down, coon. The attack's over. I figger they was just exchangin' favors, for the moment at least. . . ."

Bill Beard, crouching and darting, flung himself toward the laurels where the patrón and Jim-Bob stood.

Smell of gun smoke was heavy in the air, and the twilight reeked of quiet—as though the worlds of birds and animals and humans had all drawn in to a momentary point of stasis.

"That was them? The Hotochrukma?" Beard demanded.

"O' course it were," Flowers replied.

"Couldn't have been another bunch?"

"Not likely."

Lopez Diego cleared his throat, steadied his voice.

"I'll have a big fire built—big enough to light up half the mountain range."

"That'll help the Injuns," Flowers said, "if that's what yo're tryin' to do."

"Right, *por supuesto*. . . ."

"They rather took us by surprise," Beard remarked. "Several wounded, including some of my men. We were so damned busy hunting them, we forgot that we could be hunted just as easily. . . ."

The patrón shook his head.

"I'm not suited for this sort of command," he said. "*Desgraciadamente*, my failure to exercise effective control could have cost numerous lives. Señor Flowers, I'm in your debt. . . ."

Lopez Diego didn't wait for a response. Rather, he turned on his heel and moved off in search of his second in command.

A coyote screamed against coming darkness. A second animal, some distance away, answered. In the dark trees, rock doves nervously rattled their wings in the foliage. The westward clouds had faded to dull purple, and in the east the first two or three stars grew visible.

Leather Jackets and loggers alike were dead tired— had been looking forward to a hot meal and a few hours of sleep. But now, in the aftermath of the attack, there would be neither a regular mess nor any but snatches of sleep. Half the command at a time would stand guard through the night. The wounded would be tended to, and in the morning the pursuit of Pelican Doctor and his accursed Hotochruks would begin all over.

If the Indians couldn't be apprehended here in the mountains they knew so well, Lopez Diego reasoned, they might at least be herded away to the north, into the forest beyond the San Lorenzo and Pescadero Creek. If this could be accomplished, then his mission would be judged a success, and he and his men would be allowed to return to Monterey—possibly even to Santa Barbara, far down the coast of Alta California.

He would conclude this day's journal entry with the notation that the hostile Indians had retreated, the extent of their casualties undetermined but presumed heavy, thus leaving the Leather Jackets in control of the field of battle.

13

Where Have They Gone?

Two days later, their animals plodding along under heavy, low-hanging fog, both soldiers and shingle men arrived in Santa Cruz, empty-handed, but with Patrón Lopez Diego able to assure the authorities that the recalcitrant Indios had been engaged and driven from their village, which had been burned, in accord with directives for dealing with hostile aboriginals. The *remnant* of Pelican Doctor's force had been pursued and engaged a second time, with the Indios once more retreating. An extensive search suggested that the band had either dispersed or had been herded away northward, out of the District of Santa Cruz. Beyond question, the target indigenes had been pacified.

Furthermore, Diego made a deposition with regard to the invaluable aid rendered by Señors Olivo and Beard (gentlemen engaged in the lumber business) and their crew. The presence of the shingle mill on the upper San Lorenzo, Diego continued, should prove a deterrent to any possible Indian resettlement within the district.

He and his Leather Jackets, the captain informed Bill and Raymondo, were now to be transferred to the garrison at Monterey. Once back in the provincial capital city, the deposition written in behalf of Beard and Olivo would be placed directly into the hands of Governor Pablo Vicente de Sola.

If the congenial patrón had even the slightest inkling that he'd been practiced upon, he gave no sign of it. His gratitude for the generous assistance was quite real—so that, in some perverse fashion or another, Bill actually experienced a twinge or two of something akin to remorse.

Beard and Olivo parted from the captain, mounted their horses, and set out to rejoin Samson and the rest of the crew—the "loggers" having stopped in at Branciforte, doubtless to regale their former mates with details of the adventure just past and, needless to say, to have a drink or two. Those who had been wounded, neither seriously, would be able to show off their bandages and perhaps to elicit a few free drinks.

Not far from the mission Bill and Raymondo actually got a glimpse of their old *friend* Padre Orontes, the debauched man of the cloth engaged in taking a constitutional along the beach. Fortunately for Raymondo and Bill, the miserable priest did not see them.

"Why is he here? You suppose he's caught wind of our presence? That's all we need just now. Possibly we'll have to send someone back to do a bit of reconnaissance work. . . ."

Olivo nodded.

"We should have killed that one while we had such a fine opportunity," Raymondo mumbled. "Well, perhaps Tereza has presented him with a bastard son by now, a little *Jesus* for him to hold in slavery. You know, Bill, it was not really her fault that she became his mistress—his slut. When one is a slave, one must sometimes perform unpleasant duties."

Bill shrugged. "Time wounds all heels."

"It's the other way around—how often must I explain this thing to you, Sancho Beard?"

"Well, perhaps. It's true, I've never noticed that time has any sense of justice. Who am I to debate this matter? As usual, Raymondo Quixote, you have traditional wisdom on your side."

"Should we hire someone from Branciforte to murder Orontes? That would solve one of our problems, at least."

"Later, Ray, later. Right now we've got to locate our

wives and our father-in-law. Goddamn it, I hope they're all right."

Olivo nodded.

Patrón Lopez Diego had insisted that his men had taken serious toll of the Hotochrukma—yes, when the Leather Jackets attacked and burned the village.

The following day Beard and Olivo took their men to the redwood grove where Bill and Raymondo planned to set up the shingle mill and discovered, happily enough, that wild animals had not gotten into the chuck wagon to any great extent, although chipmunks and gray squirrels had found their way into a burlap sack of beans.

With order more or less restored (promise of a bonus, and Sam Flowers given instructions with regard to which trees were to be felled next), Raymondo and Bill rode directly back to the village site below Stone Face Falls. The place was utterly deserted—no, not utterly, for a half-grown black bear, unwilling to make acquaintance, waddled away upstream without so much as a single backward glance. Winds had blown the ashes of the lodges this way and that, in effect sweeping the meadow all but clean. Bill had an uncanny sensation that human habitation in this place had vanished long ago, and a fist of loneliness, of irrevocable loss, grew tight in his guts.

Where the hell were they?

Why hadn't they returned?

Ray and Bill stood next to the pit that had once been Pelican Doctor's lodge—their home too these several months, the place in which they'd lived in such maddening closeness to the two young women with whom they'd fallen in love and had just recently married—close, yes, but only so close. . . .

"Perhaps farther up the canyon, above the waterfall," Raymondo suggested.

"Honest to Gawd, my friend, we have no idea whether anyone was killed or wounded, and neither do we have even the slightest notion as to where Pelican Doctor might have led his people."

"But would he not at least send someone back to tell his sons-in-law where he had gone?"

"Our bride price was one of weapons. The attack Pelican Doctor feared came sooner than anyone could have expected. Maybe now that bride price has been canceled. Maybe the chief realizes someone from Santa Cruz must have tailed you and me—and so discovered his hidden village. Pelican Doctor's our friend, but his first obligation is to his people. It's possible that this contact with us, and so with the civilized world, has become the most central danger. . . ."

Without speaking further, they rode on up the creek, made their way about the falls (now at low current, with no more than a veil of water seemingly suspended from the dark stone lip), and found themselves in the upper canyon, not greatly distant from where they'd been taken prisoners by the Ohlones in what now seemed like another lifetime. The canyon, thin amber of afternoon October sunlight mingling among heavy shadows of fir and pine and redwood, was empty of any human presence other than their own.

Six weeks passed. Despite numerous attempts, neither Raymondo nor Bill was able to effect any contact with the Hotochrukma. They made special journeys to such Ohlone villages as Matala-n, Kino-te, and even Tamie-n over on the Coyote River, a northward-flowing stream that fed into the southern terminus of Bahía del San Francisco. In none of these more or less civilized Indian villages was there any word of Pelican Doctor and his people, though a boy in Tamie-n insisted that he had seen a number of wild Indians pass by that village in the middle of the night, the group moving southward.

Beard and Olivo consulted their map, shook their heads. Possibly Pelican Doctor was leading his people on an exodus, intending to cross through the hills and onward to

the San Benito or even farther to the Salinas and to the
rugged wilderness of the Ventanas—the Santa Lucia Range.
For that matter, the goal of such an exodus might well have
been to cross through the coastal mountains and venture
out onto the floor of the great inland valley of the San
Joaquin, beyond the pale of Mexican control, territory of
the wild Yokuts Indians. In that immensity of terrain, a
relatively small band of Ohlones could simply vanish—
could conceivably even cross the big valley itself to the
half-mythical Snowy Mountains beyond, thought to be miles
in height. From the crests of the mountains to the east of San
José, these *Sierra Nevada* were in fact visible when the
atmosphere was lucid, as after a general rainstorm—or so
Raymondo insisted.

   Both Ray and Bill were stunned with a sense of terrible
loss, but for the time being at least, there was nothing to be
done. There was no cure, no balm in Gilead.

They threw their full energies into the business at hand,
their compulsive and fruitless ventures over the village site
below Stone Face Falls now restricted to once each week.
With Samson Flowers acting as the bull of the woods, and
with additional financial backing (in the form of loans) from
Jean Paul Martin, the partners completed their mill in the
midst of a considerable stand of redwoods, far up on the
little San Lorenzo River, just as they'd intended all along.
With or without ownership to the land, there was no one to
say them nay. This site was nearly ideal, for as soon as the
proper machinery, circular saw, and cut-off saws could be
delivered around the Horn from the foundries of Connecticut, they'd have sufficient water power from the stream to
operate as efficiently as the best of the small mills in
Vermont, New Hampshire, or the District of Maine.

   Bundles of shingles, both redwood and cedar, were cut
and transported by means of ox-drawn wagons down to a
cove at the mouth of Gazos Creek, some thirty miles to the
north of Santa Cruz. With winch line and cradle, they were
able to sling their goods to the sandy beach adjacent to the

chosen *dog hole* of a cove, a term the boys invented, deriving from the use of steel dogs and hempen lines as a method of loading cargo.

Into this cove Jean Paul Martin's freight schooner was able to enter (despite the somewhat unpredictable tides), and cargo was hoisted aboard directly. In addition to the shingles for which they'd contracted, on speculation they sent five thousand board feet of rough-cut but merchantable redwood planking and an equal amount of fir, chiefly four-by-twelves, a full twelve feet in length, goods cut by means of a whipsaw pit they'd constructed so that one man worked from above while a second operated from below—as the logs were nudged forward to the sawyers' platforms along a somewhat primitive winch line and a set of skids. The blade of the saw worked back and forth within an oaken miter (that had to be replaced every so often) so that the sawyers were able to maintain reasonable tolerances. Planking could then be hewn fairly smooth by means of adze and drawknife.

Martin himself was aboard the schooner, and he paid on the spot with coin of the realm (silver pesos) for both the shingles and the planking as well, at the same time congratulating the partners roundly and offering a toast of twenty-year-old Scotch whiskey.

Wages, in turn, were paid out to the crew. The money indeed brightened the eyes of the men from Branciforte, and as a result four of them rode off for the purpose of getting hell-roaring drunk and never showed up in camp again. But the reputation of Olivo & Beard was growing now, and suddenly they had men riding out to the operation in search of employment—more than they needed, in fact—Mexican Spanish, Peruvians, Panamanians, and of course others of the Branciforte persuasion.

Bill and Raymondo grew fearful that Samson Flowers had become restless—and was about to act upon his announced intention of heading back to beaver country. How would they get along without the services of this eccentric individual? They'd grown to depend upon him—

almost to the point of thinking of him as the third partner in the enterprise.

And the business continued to thrive.

Then one evening after chow, Flowers sauntered over to where Bill and Raymondo were sitting, smoking pipes and relaxing.

"Been thinkin', by Gord," Flowers said. "It ain't reasonable that them Injuns o' yours ain't come back. I don't figger they lost anybody to Cap'm Diablo, so they're jest staying away on purpose. Pelican Doctor, he's probably waitin' for word from his sons-in-law, that's what I'd guess."

"We've looked everywhere," Raymondo protested.

"O' course ye ain't. That's why ye ain't found 'em. A whole village don't jest vanish, not unless they get hit by the pox. In that case, the big crows'll lead ye right to 'em."

"East," Bill suggested, "out into Yokuts territory?"

"Could be, but not likely. Injuns don't get along any better'n Whites, not when it comes to sharin' stomping grounds. I've trapped in the Big Valley. Cain't see redwood Injuns goin' where they ain't no trees at all except oaks and willows along the cricks. I figger the Ventanas. A world o' *barrancas* down thar, an' no roads an' no trails. It ain't Leather Jacket country, nor much of anyone else's now. Used to be Esselens and Salinans right on the coast, but the Spanish *civilized* 'em, ye might say. I'll ride south with ye. We'll find the Pelican an' his gang, I guarantee 'er. . . ."

"And what about our operations?" Raymondo asked. "Do we have even one dog who will herd our sheep about and force them to be virtuous in our absence?"

"If we can't round up a dog," Flowers replied, "at least we can find us a wolf or two."

"Excellent, *precioso*." Raymondo laughed. "We leave the sheep-eater to guard the sheep. . . ."

"Hell, Ray-mond," Beard said, "we've got to make the attempt. I can see Pelican Doctor and the Hotochrukma staying away for a time—maybe even until they hear from us. But you and I, we've got too much at stake. We've got to find the girls."

"Hate to say it, coons, hate to say 'er by Gord. Ye got

to look at it, though. They might be dead. That might explain why Pelican Doctor's not of a mind to make contact. . . ."

Bill's eyes met Raymondo's. Flowers had just put into words their greatest fear.

With little assurance that anything profitable would transpire in their absence, and with no real certainty they'd even have a crew upon their return, Bill and Raymondo, accompanied by Samson Flowers, rode south. In Monterey they conferred briefly with Patrón Lopez Diego, who assured them he had heard nothing further of Pelican Doctor. Then they visited Jean Paul Martin, who'd secured for them several contracts for loads of shingles and structural timbers—these to be shipped to Cabo San Lucas, at the tip of Mexican Baja California.

Flowers slipped out while the partners were discussing business matters, but an hour or so later he returned, grinning.

"Gents," he grinned, "I'm of a mind to take some of that pay you promised me. Turns out there be a leetle cantina down close to the embarcadero, an' they keep a few rooms in the back."

"Rooms for drinking?" Beard asked, raising one eyebrow.

"That an' other things. Turns out, three or four o' the prettiest fillies this child's seen in a spell are down there. Friendly as any August afternoon they are, an' the rates is reasonable."

Jean Paul Martin began to laugh.

"C'est vrai, Monsieur Flowers speaks of Hotel Batahola, the place of much commotion. Perhaps, gentilhommes, you should go with your foreman. Some music, some song, some wine, some tequila—perhaps even the company of the ladies. Friends of me, it will do you good. Loneliness can turn the heart into stone. That is something I myself know only too well."

Raymondo glanced at Bill, then at Jean Paul.

"Will you come with us, then?"

Martin smiled, shook his head.

"That part of my life, it is behind me. Oh, perhaps not. Who can say? But this evening I am expected at the governor's house. You understand?"

"Hooraw for the mountains, then!" Flowers blurted. "This child's ready to pluck him a rosebud or two."

"I do not know how many *rosebuds* one is likely to find at Hotel Batahola," Jean Paul Martin said. "Well, you three are still young. You must tend to your business, I to mine, *en vérité*."

An effeminate young man wearing a sombrero and a gray jacket fringed with black stamped his feet on the cobblestone floor of the cantina, while an overweight, middle-aged woman whose hair was streaked with white drew her fingers magically across the strings of a guitar and sang Spanish love songs in a voice that seemed strangely small and delicate, considering the lady's ample proportions. The customers, all of them apparently members of the well-to-do class, the *Gente de Razón*, clapped their hands and occasionally raised their drinks and whistled.

Beard, Olivo, and Flowers made their way to the bar and seated themselves.

"*Tomar una copita, señors?*"

"*Vino tintro,*" Olivo replied.

"And the señoritas," Flowers added quickly. "This child's looking for a fe-male companyero."

The barkeep glanced at the three men—one dressed in workman's clothing and clearly out of place.

"*Mucho dinero,*" the barkeep said.

Flowers laughed. "Sure enough, sure enough. Speak English, damn yore soul."

Beard and Olivo shook their heads, signifying no desire for a consort.

The barkeep brought a pitcher of red wine and four glasses. He filled all of them and then tapped his fingers on the bar.

"We must rent a *puta* for our guide?" Raymondo asked Bill.

"Looks that way."

Beard paid the barkeep his money.

"Thank ye, thank ye," Flowers said, raising his glass. "Summat to drink and a soft leetle señorita for Samson, and I'll find ye them Hotochruks right off. Won't take long, I give you my word. The ladies always want it to last longer'n it does, but they ain't no reason to try to please 'em. Hellfire an' damnation, if I ever thought a fee-male was actually startin' to enjoy gettin' humped, I'd stop right then an' thar."

"An enlightened point of view," Raymondo said. "Long ago you taught me to shoe a horse, Señor Flowers, and now you instruct me in the proper ways of making love. *Gracias, gracias!*"

At this point an attractive young Indio woman appeared. She was dressed in a short bouffant skirt of bright yellow linen and an elaborately embroidered blouse, light blue, with puffy sleeves reaching down to her forearms. On her left wrist were several silver bracelets, one of which sported a considerable lump of polished turquoise. Her long hair, cinched behind her head with a wooden comb, glistened in the candlelight and fell to her waist.

It was none other than Tereza, the girl Orontes had taken as a plaything at the San Gabriel Mission—and for whom, directly or indirectly, Raymondo had received his brutal flogging.

For her part, Tereza (number 1002 on the San Gabriel rolls) smiled mechanically and started to ask the gentlemen if she might be blessed with a taste of red wine—when her words broke off in mid-sentence. For a long moment she stared directly at the expressionless Olivo.

"Little Fish Eagle, Raymondo, is that you?" she managed at last. "Padre Orontes told us that you and Señor Barrington had been apprehended and hanged. . . ."

"*A fortunado*, I am still among the living. What are you doing in this place, Tereza?"

The young woman smiled pleasantly then, her composure restored.

"I take gentlemen to my room, and they pay me well, *desde luego*. I have worked here for two months now—I am *La Belle du Soir*. Will you be my partner, Raymondo, or do all three of you wish to join me? I would like that, but it will cost more. . . ."

"Know the gal, do ye?" Flowers laughed. "Ye want to go first, be my guest. Billy an' me, we'll get drunk while we're waitin'."

Beard shook his head. He was mostly of a mind to walk out of the place—stroll back to Jean Paul's and get a few hours of shut-eye.

"Ah, Tereza! It is sad, sad, *melancólico* to find you here. Once I loved you, but now . . . Go with my friend, Señor Flowers. He will treat you well. . . ."

Tereza studied the three men, moved her head with the comeliness of a healthy young mare, and smiled brilliantly. She drank her glass of wine, touched a single finger to her lips, and extended her hand toward Samson Flowers.

"Please," she said, "you must pay me before we go to the *dormitorio*. You will see that I am worth the fee. I will do whatever you wish me to, and after that you will come to visit me again and again. . . . And you will tell your friend Raymondo that I am very good at what I do."

Flowers rose, took Tereza's hand, and winked at Bill and Raymondo. Then he and Tereza walked off, arm in arm, toward a curtained archway.

Beard shrugged at Olivo and gazed across the room to where the thin-featured young man was performing a bullfighter's dance, complete with bells and castanets. The overweight woman, no longer singing, her eyes closed, caused her guitar to wail like a creature in either pain or ecstasy.

"Fortune is a strange thing," Raymondo said as he drank his wine. "In the course of a lifetime, we are expected to play many different roles. Possibly Tereza will end up marrying someone who will eventually become governor of all of California. Who can say?"

"It does not bother you—seeing her go off with Samson?"

"Ah, companyero," Raymondo smiled sadly, "you and I, we are married men. Unfortunately, we do not at the moment have any idea where our wives are—or even, for that matter, whether they are still alive."

"We'll find the Pelican Doctor's people, Ray. With Sam Flowers to lead us, how can we go wrong?"

Raymondo poured another glass of wine.

"I wish you had not put it quite that way, *mi Sancho* . . . ."

With first light they rode on southward, past the Carmel Mission and Point Lobos and on toward the Ventana Mountains, blue in the distance. They forded Mal Paso Creek and continued their journey along the coast beneath the mass of Mount Carmel, passing inland of Palo Colorado and Point Sur and on to Rio Sur Grande. Here, close by the river's mouth, they camped for the night.

Sunset flared an astonishing redness across the western sky as heavy stormclouds moved in. A warm wind was blowing, and the horses were uneasy.

"Goin' to be a humdinger," Flowers said as the three of them hovered about their fire pit—in an attempt to protect the struggling flames from gusts of wind that sent curtains of loose sand singing up over the dunes.

They set a coffeepot to brewing and ate cold meat and dark bread smeared with butter. When the coffee was ready and the men attempted to pour the steaming liquid into pewter cups, wind vaporized most of it. They held their hands about their cups and gulped the coffee. Then bands of lightning began to flash, and the heavy sound of thunder battered the gaining darkness.

"Let's string up the slicker," Beard said. "Rain—rain's going to be pouring down in a minute."

"Wind'll blow 'er away," Flowers countered. "Best we

move upstream—find us some big redwoods for cover. . . ."

"*Santa ternera!*" Raymondo cried. "Wind'll blow us away! It is two or three miles back to the groves."

Immense flashes of lightning, ear-splitting noise.

And rain.

A downpour.

The horses snorted and stamped about in outrage, and Beard, Olivo, and Flowers resorted to huddling together beneath some lupine bushes, their slicker pulled about them.

"Had better company last night," Flowers grumbled.

At some time past midnight the rain left off. The members of the search party struggled to get a fire going once more, but all available fuel was soaked. Beard fetched the shingling hatchet from his soggy saddlebags and split and made shavings of a chunk of driftwood. Finally a little fire was burning, and the men huddled about it. They got out their jug of *aguardiente* and passed it back and forth, grateful for the strong drink.

The earth heaved beneath their feet, and a thirty-foot sand dune behind them lurched forward in the darkness.

Earthquake.

In the distance a deep ripping, crashing sound was followed by a long, surging roar.

"Half the mountain has come down!" Beard shouted. "Jesus Kee-rhyste!"

"Perhaps it is time for Coyote to make the world over again," Olivo said. "The elements, they are telling us to go back to San Lorenzo River. Or perhaps the Great Dreamer has awakened."

Beard laughed. "Could have been God's own redwood fell over."

"No redwood is that big," Olivo admitted. "Next we will have either a great forest fire, or a tidal wave will come in from the Pacific."

"Now that ye mention 'er," Flowers said, "the Gord-damn tide's goin' out in a hell of a hurry. What's that mean, Beard?"

"It means," Bill Beard replied, "that we've got to get

the hell away from this beach as fast as we can move. That jolt in the earth—it's subject to bring a tsunami in on top of us. Let's move out!"

Flowers cursed. He couldn't find the coffeepot. Sand from the dune had slid down and covered the fire pit. Even the slicker was half covered.

"To hell with it!" Beard yelled. "Where are the horses?"

As if in response, the animals began to snort and whinny.

The three men mounted and lurched ahead in the darkness, urging their ponies to move more rapidly than they wished to. They traversed over dunes of wet sand and finally upslope, away from the shore.

Behind them the muted sound of a great surge of water, of small trees snapping, of rocks and sand in motion, of boulders grinding against boulders.

14

Bill the Sawyer

The search party moved away from the coast, back into the recesses of the Ventanas, marble foreheads rising precipitously from the heaving Pacific. They moved carefully, searching watershed after watershed and working their way toward the backs of the mountains and the hot springs at Tassajara. During the following three days numerous shivers went through the earth. Beard made note that each occasion was preceded by an absence of bird song—so that he was actually able to predict the last two aftershocks thirty minutes or so before the tremors occurred.

"Coyote brings the mountains up out of the sea," Raymondo said. "Eventually he will take them back down again. Maybe he's thinking about such a reversal of the old order right now."

"You sure it ain't big redwoods going over?" Beard asked.

"Most likely Pelican Doctor'll be on the move too," Flowers said as they rested their ponies on a high oak and pine-studded ridge above Tassajara. "Might of gone south already—down into the Santa Lucias or over onto the Nacimiento River. The mountains get barren as you move inland, so I don't figger they've gone too far. The San Benitos is east of here, to the other side of Salinas River, but that jest ain't their kind of country."

Beard gazed off toward the north, where a pair of huge-winged condors floated effortlessly against blazing blue sky. Even at so great a distance the king-birds looked *big*.

"When people are on the run," Beard suggested, "the *right kind* of country is empty country—as far from the Leather Jackets as possible. Protecting the people from the Leather Jackets—it's an obsession with the old chief, and rightly so. Hell, maybe they've joined forces with the Yokuts. . . ."

"We've found nothing, no trace even," Olivo said. "Yet it's not possible for them simply to have disappeared."

"If a coon knows the land good enough," Flowers said, leaning forward to rub his pony behind the ears, "he can damn near *disappear*. Pelican Doctor didn't stay chief so long by being stupid in the head. . . ."

Olivo and Beard exchanged wordless glances.

They had brought weapons to their father-in-law, but perhaps they'd inadvertently brought the soldiers as well. Possibly Pelican Doctor had now decided simply to cut all ties with his sons-in-law—to cut ties and to venture into the uninhabited interior—uninhabited at least by Californios. . . .

They camped that night high on the northern shoulder of Junipero Serra Peak, overlooking Tassajara. They'd followed a dry arroyo up on the mountain—because the pathway along the ravine indicated fairly heavy foot traffic; yes, and recently. Where the ravine opened out into some sheltered meadows, they found certain evidence of an encampment—but one that had been abandoned perhaps a week earlier.

There was nothing in particular to indicate the Indians had been Hotochruks.

As the fire dwindled to red coals and the night air grew chilly, Bill Beard lay in his bedroll and recalled the singular story Seagull had told him—of the man who'd sought after his wife even in death.

Was that, for all practical purposes, what he himself

was now doing? Was it possible that she was simply *gone*?

No. He couldn't accept it. Every fiber of his being cried out for his wife. Countless stars burned down out of the sable darkness, and across the meadows where lately an Indian village had stood, crickets made constant chorus.

"We'll find them, *hermano*," Raymondo said, his voice barely more than a whisper. "Eventually Pelican Doctor will come searching for us. Where would he ever find two other such sons-in-law as us?"

"Mebbe that's why he's on the run," Flowers growled. "Gord damn it, go to sleep. . . ."

Beard chuckled. "Our friend forgets that we're his employers. And that means we have the right to talk all night, if we wish."

"This child'll club the two o' ye to death if he has to," Flowers insisted. "A man needs to sleep, eat, drink, an' fornicate, in that order, if he wants to stay healthy an' keep a sane mind. Do I got to go up on the mountain to get away from all this jabber, or what?"

"Be quiet," Raymondo hissed, "you're keeping me awake."

The voices ceased, but still Beard did not sleep. He stared at the heavens and listened to the shrill chitter of crickets. Then he closed his eyes, breathed deeply, savoring the odors of the forest—odors that yet suggested human presence. Just as he drifted into sleep, he was half certain he'd detected that strange, clean, faint, exciting smell of his wife's presence.

Then he dreamed.

He was with Seagull—just the two of them together—and it was as though none of all this had ever happened. Indeed, Gull didn't seem aware of the battles, although when he brought up the matter, asking where the Hotochrukma had gone, she laughed as though she had some mischievous secret.

"I have told you about Coyote, my husband. Coyote likes to gamble. So does Eagle, Redtail, Puma, Weasel, Gray Fox, and Redhead Woodpecker. They were all hunt-

ers, and they went out for rabbits. Afterward they gave
the intestines to Coyote so that he could breathe on
them and turn them into rabbits once more. There must
always be rabbits so that the hunters will have something to
eat."

"Why are you telling me this?" Beard asked his wife.

"You ask too many questions. That's probably because
you came from Vermont. Americans always wish to know
why things happen. Listen now. The hunters began to
gamble—I think they were playing the hand game, each one
trying to guess which hand the other used to hold the small
carved bone. Then a Black-eared Rabbit came in.
He complained that the hunters were always after his
children. He said if they were hungry, he'd give them good
things to eat. So he gave them pine nuts and bags full of
blackberries and sweet roots. After that the hunters decided Black-eared Rabbit was a good fellow. Now they
wished him to play the hand game with them. Rabbit liked
that idea, and he began to win. He kept winning until he
had won everything.

"Coyote was watching, but he didn't join the gambling.
He just gave everyone else good advice. Sometimes Coyote
does that. So he suggested they wait for the next day and
then gamble some more. That's what they did, and this time
Redtail won everything back from Black-eared Rabbit. The
Rabbit said he had nothing left, but Redtail said he should
cut off his ear and play with that. The Rabbit agreed, but
Coyote said to wait. He'd be right back.

"Coyote went to his own lodge and asked his wife to
give him his magic ball, but his wife said she didn't know
where it was. Coyote told her it was under the pillow. . . ."

"Damn it, Gull," Beard protested, "don't you realize
that I've searched everywhere for you? I've gone back to the
village again and again, and now I'm way down here in the
Ventana Mountains. . . ."

"You haven't looked everywhere, William Hair-on-his
Face. You haven't looked in the places where we have been.
I wish you'd come to me. Do you not realize that our

*children are growing within my body? I wish you'd come to
me, my husband. I'm not like that woman who had to pass
between the huge stones into Other Side Camp."*

"You're still alive? You promise me that?"

*"Yes. Now listen to the rest of my story. You're worse
than an impatient child, William Beard. This is what
happened. Coyote lifted the pillow and showed his wife the
magic ball was there, just as he said. Then, when she leaned
over to look at the ball, he pushed her down on the bed and
jumped on top of her and slid his long penis into her. His
wife growled at him and said that was all he was ever
interested in—and why did he suppose he had to fool her
into lying down with him? Coyote told her he was trying to
help Black-eared Rabbit, so that he wouldn't have to cut off
his ears. The wife said all right, hurry up then. And Coyote
did."*

"I know this story has a point," Beard said.

*"Of course it does. Whitemen are always too impatient.
The Coyote got up off his wife and shook his fur and then
went back to where the gamblers were. Now Black-eared
Rabbit was winning again, and so he didn't have to cut off
his ears after all. He was winning all of Redtail's shell
money. Coyote grinned and asked how the gambling was
going."*

"And the point is? The moral of the story?"

*Seagull put her arms around him and pressed her head
against him. She bit at the hair on his chest. "Coyote has
strange ways," she said. "But sometimes he makes things
happen the way they should. . . ."*

Beard awoke. He was short of breath. For a moment
he was certain Seagull was there with him—or that she'd
just now risen and would return to his side momentarily.

A waning moon hung in the sky, and the broad
meadow at the edge of the forest glittered.

Did he detect an odor of smoke in the air? Smoke,
perhaps, from campfires other than their own?

A screech owl trilled the sharp, lonely trill of its mating
call—repeated the sequence of notes over and over, but no
other bird called out in answer. Dawn would not come for

another two or three hours, and Beard resolved to sleep some more. The fruitless search had gone on long enough. In the morning they'd cook breakfast, eat, and then begin the long ride back toward the Sierra Santa Cruz and San Lorenzo River.

All things were in Coyote's hands, or paws, as the case might be. Surely the Hotochrukma would reappear. Life without his woman, Beard concluded, would be empty, meaningless.

"Goddamn it, Gull," he whispered, "you got no business running off this way. You being gone—it's like a fist inside me. It hurts, damn it, it hurts."

If this land of Alta California were, so to speak, Eden itself, then both he and Raymondo had been cast into exile. The shimmer of beauty, the *shine*, to use Sam Flowers' term, had vanished.

With the next arrival of Martin's "dog-hole schooner," came a mysterious message demanding the immediate appearance in Monterey of both Señor Beard and Señor Olivo, posthaste. Martin himself was not on board, but the captain of the scow was quite definite in his directions. Bill and Raymondo were not to accompany the ship south but rather to take to their horses and proceed to Monsieur Martin's establishment as quickly as possible.

With Flowers in charge of all operations, Bill and Raymondo left their logging woods behind and rode toward the small capital city of California. Two days later they found themselves in the company of Jean Paul Martin as they presented themselves at the mansion of Governor Pablo Vicente de Sola—yes, invited to dine as honored guests of the great man and his wife.

In recompense for the good-Samaritan-like services in assisting Patrón Lopez Diego and the Leather Jackets in their attempt to quell the uprising of a rebel band of Santa Cruz Ohlone Indians, and further as a means of encouraging local entrepreneurial undertakings and of helping to create a base for local industry, Spanish authorities, via the person of Governor Sola, had looked favorably upon the petition for a land grant. Suddenly Olivo and Beard had been admitted to the gentry, with thirty-two thousand acres of forest entitled in their behalf, much of it in redwoods, at their disposal. The partners were, in short, the bona fide owners of Rancho San Lorenzo.

Great Gawd!

Fate's huge dice had been cast without their even knowing it, and somehow, miraculously, what had been no more than a pipe dream hatched by an Ohlone serf and a Vermont merchant marine deserter, hatched in fact while the two were in the act of cleaning the stables of Padre Orontes, had now become a sufficient reality so that one could easily project a virtual empire and a great fortune to match—given merely the requisites of sufficient time and good health.

The irony of the damned thing . . . In attempting to protect Pelican Doctor's people, they'd actually assisted in driving the Hotochrukma out of the area—and with them, needless to say, the two young women to whom their wretched hearts were devoted.

With some men, no doubt, the prospect of wealth served to obliterate the need for romantic satisfaction, and money itself became the Divine Mistress. Individual females, like other kinds of property, were simply commodities to be enjoyed at leisure and then put aside. For others, however, *affairs of the heart* rendered all other considerations extraneous.

What good was a dream without the woman for whom one dreamed? Raymondo and Bill agreed that whatever level of success they might accomplish would be mere emptiness, mere show, without Seagull and Calling Owl. Could prestige and wealth actually provide a balm, a solace? Ray and Bill mulled the question. A further interesting consideration of values: were wealth and property even necessary to the leading of the good life? Possibly the manner in which the companyeros defined *good* was far different than would have been the case for two gentlemen of sound mind.

Into Beard's thoughts came the momentary image of Christie O'Brien, but with the image came no sense of regret. Nothing but a memory, a recollection devoid of any emotion beyond a mere reflection upon passing time, of one life, one world swallowing all that had gone before. Would time, equally, serve to obliterate the keen joy he'd had of Seagull? Was that possible?

P'an' tanzhi. The year has passed. Once again the acorns have fallen. The old world has fallen away. . . .

For Raymondo and Bill, it was maddening not to know, at the very least, whether Seagull and Calling Owl were yet alive. The partners returned again and again to the vicinity of the Hotochruk site, but the redwood glades and the meadows beside Big Creek remained strangely, vexingly empty. In the canyon above, that stone face in whose honor Pelican Doctor's people had named the falls continued to stare mournfully northward—as if to suggest this particular sacred direction might somehow offer up the vital clue necessary to the solution of the mystery: where were Pelican Doctor and his people?

Again and again in his dreams, Bill Beard found himself with Seagull, and the two of them walked beside the heaving ocean or sat in the pleasant shade of great redwood trees, conversing with one another and loving each other as though nothing whatsoever had happened.

Beautiful Seagull, woman whose voice is like the flowing of clear water over bright pebbles, whose long hair is a silent storm around her shoulders, whose eyes meet mine so that we know one another in a way that only we ourselves will ever understand. What force has taken you from me? What evil fate has conspired against us? And how am I left to live the remainder of my life without my dearly beloved, my closest woman friend, mi alma? Do not stay away any longer, Seagull! Even though you come to me in my dreams, that is not enough. I must know if you still breathe the air, if your gleaming eyes still configure the shimmering sunlight into images—I must

know this, even though it were death to discover
you dead. Once you told me the tale of a man who
attempted to follow his dead wife into the Spirit World,
and how he was able to slip through that passageway
between huge, crashing boulders—how he gained permis-
sion from the Chief of the Spirit World to take his wife with
him back into the land of the living—yes, and how his
desire for her foiled his plans. But then he himself was
found dead, and so his spirit must have joined hers at
last. . . . That man was fortunate. At least he knew and
therefore was granted a course of action. Seagull, are you
out there somewhere in the forest? Have you gone north or
south? Or east, perhaps, into the great valley of the San
Joaquin? Send me some message—let the cries of the jay
and the high, distant flight of the condor tell me where to
search for you. . . .

What passed for winter along the coast of Alta California
came and went, bringing with it occasional heavy rain-
storms with temperate intervals in between and no more
than half a dozen separate days when frost actually formed,
whitening the sword ferns and the forest duff and producing
a glaze on the water in puddles. Twice the highest peaks in
the Santa Cruz Mountains blazed white with newfallen
snow, whiteness that nonetheless vanished within a day or
so.

Operations at the mill site were going quite well,
though Bill fully expected with the coming of spring to see
Samson Flowers riding off and signaling farewell with a
wave of his Hawken flintlock.

The partners now had fifty men working for them, and
from time to time new equipment arrived from Mexico,
with the assistance of Jean Paul Martin, of course, since
without his aid nothing of the sort could ever have happened. For reasons he never in fact shared with Beard and
Olivo, the keen-eyed Frenchman who'd chosen to expatri-
ate himself from his own country in the aftermath of his
nation's *Grand Revolution for liberty, equality, and*

fraternity—complete with the methodical siren song of *La Guillotine* and the consequent rise and fall of the Little Corporal—Jean Paul Martin had taken Beard and Olivo under his wing and supplied both the credit and the influence necessary to the furtherance of their operations.

But despite everything, a terrible heaviness hung like a pall over all their gains, all their successes—for they were still without word as to either the whereabouts or the fate of the women they'd taken to wife.

And the course of the year swung back to equinox, to vernal equinox and the season of regeneration, of resurrection.

Vice-gerent of the Divine, Lord of Life reascendant, green flux of creation itself. . . .

Beard's yearning for Seagull, or at the very least for knowledge of her fate, hadn't grown less sharp as the months passed, one after another, though perhaps he'd come to accept the inevitable. Somehow, even in the face of what seemed to him the greatest of tragedies, he managed to stumble forward, to plant one foot after another and to continue in the path he and Raymondo had set for themselves.

Whether his friend was in fact more accepting of fate, Beard was largely unable to determine. Raymondo went about his business, uncomplaining. But the laugh lines about his eyes had seemingly vanished.

When pressed at one point, Raymondo said simply, "Tío coyote, he has whims. He does not truly mean us any harm, *mi hermano*, and yet we cannot trust him either. It's the same with the wind or the great waves that sometimes rise up out of the sea itself."

So it was that Bill and Raymondo managed to push ahead with the business of the mill; and to this end they'd ridden south to Monterey. They were at Martin's residence once again, the three men going over the records and discussing possibilities for new and expanded ventures. Jean Paul, quite pleased with himself, presented a crate to Raymondo—a crate that proved to be filled with books, some eighteen of them, to be precise. Among these was Virgil's *Aenead* translated into Spanish, Pope's version of Homer's *Iliad* and *Odyssey*, Shakespeare's complete plays in their original English, and Racine's *Phaedra* in French, the book full-bound in split leather, its title embossed and its edges in gold.

The volumes, worth a small fortune, had been part of an inheritance—and now the gift of one lover of the printed word to another.

Raymondo, bookworm that he was, stood all but tongue-tied. The man was stunned by the nature of this generous present—for here, after all, was the core of what might eventually become the considerable little library for which he had long expressed a desire.

"I've never known a man," William Beard nodded, "to be so *queer for books* as Raymondo Olivo."

"Maintenant," Jean Paul remarked as he lit his briar, "since we have concluded all our necessary transactions, it's possible I have some news for you gentlemen. However ill-advised it may have been for you to wed women from an uncivilized and wild tribe, still I believe I understand what it's like to be deprived of the company of one's beloved. What I'm about to speak is rumor only, mind you, and the wise man learns not to base his life on such sources of information. Nevertheless, I've learned that contact has been made with a new Indian village far back up into the Santa Lucia Mountains. My informant, *un homme* whose word I have no reason to doubt, refers to these Indians as *Hoot-chukkars.* At first I supposed the name to be no more than a combination of the sound of an owl and the name of a grouse. Only later did the similarity of syllables actually occur to me—*Hoot-chukkars* and *Hotochrukma.* I appreciate fully the heartbreak you two have experienced, and so possibly this clue is something you should follow up on—for your own peace of mind, at the very least."

Martin's words indeed registered their impact on both Bill's psyche and Raymondo's. With the first light of dawn, the owners of Rancho San Lorenzo were again riding south-ward, a pair of pack animals in tow behind them. They forded Carmel River and proceeded along the coast to Mal Paso Creek and Garrapatas Creek and on to the first of the Sur rivers, the Sur Límitado, where they turned inland, following now the general course of the small stream and then up its south fork.

As the journey continued, Beard and Olivo did indeed discover signs of Indian habitation, but the dark redwood forests and then, farther along, the groves of firs and pines and hedges of liveoak and willow were alive merely with the songs of real birds. The screech owl didn't trill at the wrong time of day, nor did the coyote yip its warning to those in the village.

The riders passed over the crest of the range and, as twilight deepened, made their way down into a forested valley beneath a peak they took to be one of the Ventana cones. A good-sized creek tumbled from the mountain (where a bit of snow was still visible by late afternoon sunlight), a stream they surmised to be the upper reaches of Carmel River itself.

The partners pitched their camp, in the process build-ing up the fire until it was much larger than needed, though the spring night was somewhat chilly. In this particular case they were actually desirous of being discovered by the mysterious *Hoot-chukkars*, whoever they might be.

Bill and Ray ate their evening meal, listened reflec-tively to the repeated cries of a mourning dove (as they imagined) calling for his mate, and then, following a long conversation in which they essentially defined the entirety of their relationship with the Hotochrukma in general and with Seagull and Calling Owl in particular, they slept.

When morning sun awoke them, the two men were disappointed to discover no band of tattooed warriors surrounding them, no thick-necked, barrel-chested chief.

They continued their search for an additional two days. Aside from the discovery of a village site which had been occupied within the recent past, however, all efforts proved

fruitless. As a matter of fact, Beard and Olivo made actual
contact with not so much as a single Indian of any
persuasion—just as had been the case when they'd ridden
south in the company of Samson Flowers. At length, as if
finally realizing the folly of attempting to recapture that
which was gone out of their lives forever, they turned
their horses northward and made their way across the
Sierra de Salinas and on toward Santa Cruz and Rancho San
Lorenzo.

It was perhaps half an hour after quitting time at the mill.

"Hoorah, coons!" Samson Flowers sang out as Olivo
and Beard rode up to the knot of men gathered about the
boeuf du bois, who was regaling the boys with a story about
how Charbonneau once arm-wrestled a grizzly bear and
actually won, even though the bear elected to operate by
Texas rules. "By Gord, it's themselves, Señor Raymond and
Señor Bill the Sawyer. I was planning to set out tomorrow
morning to discover if ye two thieves was dead or just
sleeping off a powerful drunk somewhere. Truth is, I'm
about to head for the beaver grounds myself, an' I wanted
to say good-bye an' thank ye. It's against nature for a man to
spend all his time cutting down trees, an' that's a sartin
fact."

Raymondo and Bill dismounted.

Something about the way Samson had spoken suggested that, in fact, he meant exactly what he said—and the
partners were going to have to find someone else to be their
head honcho and chief bottle washer.

Flowers clasped Beard's hand and proceeded to pound
Olivo on the back.

"Like I jest told ye, gents, I'm fixing to ride north to
Nez Percé country directly. Would have gone already.
Know how it is—when the time comes 'round, a man's
obliged to follow where the Big Coyote leads. But first I
wanted to see the expressions on your faces when ye
discovered the damned mill site's been invaded by a whole
pack of red divvils. . . ."

Samson Flowers threw back his shaggy head and roared with laughter.

"What in hell? Where?" Beard demanded.

"Jest over to the other side o' the mill, naturally, ye bull's pizzle."

Bill and Raymondo were running. It took nearly forever to cover that interval of no more than a hundred yards—and then the partners saw them: Pelican Doctor himself and his beautiful twin daughters, Seagull and Calling Owl. *Gull! Gull! Curse my soul, but it's actually you!*

Samson Flowers rode off into the forest and didn't return, but the operations of Olivo & Beard continued to thrive. Raymondo Olivo and Guillermo Beard were well on their way to becoming wealthy men, and at midsummer of that year, 1818, almost precisely nine months after Ray and Bill had taken them to wife, Seagull and Calling Owl gave birth to children—Calvin and Califia, twin son and daughter to Seagull and William Beard—and Homer Virgil, a son to Calling Owl and Raymondo Olivo.

Just before Christmas of that year, word was received that Padre Orontes had been found dead in the Santa Cruz retreat house, apparently due to some sort of seizure or heart attack. The priest hadn't been alone at the time of his death. A young Indio girl, perhaps no more than fourteen years old (according to rumor) was found in hysterical condition, chained to the priest's bed. The young woman, as matters turned out, was never prosecuted for murder.

It was said that one of the other priests accepted the obligation of caring for the girl's immortal soul—and in fact had taken her south with him, on a venture to Santa Barbara.

ABOUT THE AUTHOR

BILL HOTCHKISS was born in Connecticut in 1936, the elder son of William Henry Hotchkiss and Merle Bertha [Stambaugh] Hotchkiss. At the conclusion of World War Two, the family moved to the West Coast, first to Medford, Oregon, and finally to Grass Valley, California, in the Mother Lode Region. Here the author grew up, attending public schools and graduating from high school in 1954.

A university scholarship and summer employment with the U.S. Forest Service took him to U.C. Berkeley and a B.A. in English in 1959. The following year he received an M.A. from San Francisco State University, and further graduate work led to M.F.A., D.A., and Ph.D., all in English, from the University of Oregon.

Hotchkiss and his wife, poet and novelist Judith Shears, live in seclusion either in Woodpecker Ravine, near the end of an unpaved former logging road, some eight miles from the town of Grass Valley, California, or, alternately, on Munger Creek, near the metropolis of Williams, Oregon, in the Siskiyous. Their present menagerie consists of two dozen or so bantam cross chickens, a pair of button quail, three domestic turkeys, two wild turkeys found hitch hiking near Siskiyou Pass, six cats, three dogs, a skunk that persists in living under the house, and several Steller's jays whose job it is to harvest cherries, in season. Visitors include a pair of pileated woodpeckers who are fond of dogwood berries, a young doe who used to live in the house but who has now liberated herself into the wild and returns sometimes at night to eat dry dog food, a flock of approximately thirty crows who roost in a nearby Douglas fir, and an occasional raven, coyote, or porcupine—the latter engaging in some sort of perverse professional arrangement with the three aforementioned dogs.

The stirring novel of a family who lived and worked among California's magnificent redwoods—and changed history forever...

TO FELL
THE GIANTS

Bill Hotchkiss

The untouched beauty of California's forests and rivers was before them; they came to the land with a bold dream of felling the giant redwoods, centuries old, to build a profitable industry. But the dream had perils and repercussions—and raised questions that live on in our hearts and minds today. Would their success stand the test of time? Or would future generations pay the price for felling the giants with a ravaged, once-glorious land? Follow the power and passion of one remarkable family and explore how the bold intentions of California's earliest settlers changed our lives forever—in a sweeping novel of power and brilliance.

TERRY C. JOHNSTON

Winner of the prestigious Western Writer's award, Terry C. Johnston brings you his award-winning saga of mountain men Josiah Paddock and Titus Bass who strive together to meet the challenges of the western wilderness in the 1830's.

☐ 25572-X **CARRY THE WIND–Vol. I** $5.50

☐ 26224-6 **BORDERLORDS–Vol. II** $5.50

☐ 28139-9 **ONE-EYED DREAM–Vol. III** $4.95

The final volume in the trilogy begun with *Carry the Wind* and *Borderlords*, ONE-EYED DREAM is a rich, textured tale of an 1830's trapper and his protegé, told at the height of the American fur trade.

Following a harrowing pursuit by vengeful Arapaho warriors, mountain man Titus "Scratch" Bass and his apprentice Josiah Paddock must travel south to old Taos. But their journey is cut short when they learn they must return to St. Louis…and old enemies.